"We are embarking on our honeymoon, remember?"

"I—I trusted you," Melly broke in.

"*Mon Dieu,* you really do have a phobia about men, don't you?" Jourdan looked exasperated.

She didn't answer him. Her heart was thudding, and she was seeing images that tortured her, brought sharply into focus by her realization that no marriage could be really impersonal.

"Melly, you are behaving as if I've committed a crime!" Jourdan took hold of her hand. "I'm not going to force myself on you."

She tried to pull free. "You've gone and spoiled things, and you were the one who promised...."

His eyes scoured her tear-wet face. "I feel I have the right to share whatever it is that puts that look in your eyes."

She ached with the misery of not being able to confide in him. Her secret was one she couldn't share with Jourdan...no, never with him!

Secret Fire

Violet Winspear

Harlequin Books

TORONTO • NEW YORK • LONDON
AMSTERDAM • PARIS • SYDNEY • HAMBURG
STOCKHOLM • ATHENS • TOKYO • MILAN

Original hardcover edition published in 1984
by Mills & Boon Limited

ISBN 0-373-02682-X

Harlequin Romance first edition March 1985

CHAPTER ONE

MELLY didn't see the new patient for several days, but she knew the nurses were in a flutter over him.

She had to smile quietly to herself; if he was so fascinating then it was just as well that she had been on hand to help save his life. Her blood group was also Tj (a) negative and she had been his donor.

It wasn't until he was allowed to eat again and she entered his room, carrying in the tray with his spartan lunch, that she understood why he had caused the nurses to have raised temperatures. He lay there in bed, arms and torso bare against the white sheets, scrolled black hair centred to a peak above eyes that watched her all the way to his bedside.

Melly summoned a smile, but she found him intimidating. She felt a force in him, something proud and arresting. Under his intent gaze she felt as if her nerves had touched a live wire.

'What have you brought me, a large juicy steak?' His voice was deep, gritty and foreign.

'You'd be lucky, Mr Lanier. It's chicken broth and noodles for you, with a slice of Melba toast.'

'Ah, I shall no doubt get fat on such a repast.' He eased himself into a sitting position and as Melly placed the tray on the bed-table she could see the hard definition of his muscles beneath the deeply tanned skin. Jourdan Lanier wasn't exactly handsome, but he had a potent masculinity; the air of a man in charge of his own destiny.

'I suppose you wouldn't care to feed me?' He ran his eyes over her face and hair. 'All that surgery has left me feeling somewhat lazy.'

'You've strength enough to pick up a spoon,' she retorted. 'I've other lunches to serve and wasn't sent in here to be your maid.'

'Such a pity.' He tasted the soup. 'Mmm, needs a dash of pepper.'

'Then blow on it,' Melly murmured.

He spooned soup and fixed her with grey eyes of an almost shocking attraction in his hard, distinctive face. 'You are not a London girl, are you?'

She shook her head. 'I come from Devonshire, from a sleepy little village which hasn't changed in centuries.'

'I thought your voice had a touch of Devon cream in it—ah, you look surprised. Did you think a Frenchman couldn't know about such choice dishes as the cream and strawberries of Devonshire? What I would not give for such a dessert right now, but instead you bring me a slice of toast.' He flicked a piece of it into his mouth, crunching it with teeth as firm as his shoulders.

'Young woman, you must find London very noisy after growing up in the countryside?'

'I've grown used to the faster pace of life in the city, and there's compensation in being able to see all the new shows and films.'

'And I bet you go for the love and romance, eh?'

'And what's wrong with that?' She flushed uncontrollably.

'Not a thing—it makes the world go round.'

From where Melly stood he looked as if he had been on that roundabout more than once, and she was turning away from his bed when he asked: 'Are you the young woman who gave me the transfusion?'

She nodded. 'I'm glad it helped you.'

'So am I,' he said whimsically. 'So you and I have something in common?'

'Yes, Mr Lanier.' She made for the door. 'Eat up all your broth, won't you?'

'So I shall be big and strong again? Don't go for a minute!'

'I have my work to do——'

'Allow me to thank you, you doubtless saved my life.'

'I'm sure it was worth saving, Mr Lanier.'

'It is generous of you to say so—Melly.'

She gave him a quick, uncertain look ... she supposed he had persuaded Sister Hope to tell him the name of the Good Samaritan who had supplied the blood transfusion.

'I really must go.' Melly gave him a tentative smile. 'I wish you well, sir.'

'I hope that Melly isn't a diminutive of Melisande?'

'Why?' Melly was caught in the strongest current of wanting to hurry away from him and wanting to stay so she could look at him and listen to him speaking in his deep Latin voice, using English words in a way she had never heard before, so they acquired deeper shades of meaning.

'Melisande was a very wicked lady, so a name like that would not be suitable for such as you.' A smile quirked his lip. 'Do I guess that it's

Melanie, the shy young thing with the doe-like eyes who took Ashley Wilkes from the scorching Scarlett O'Hara—I, too, see the occasional film, you see?'

'Well, that isn't my name, Mr Lanier.' Melly had to admire his persistence. 'I wasn't named after a character in *Gone With The Wind*.'

'Then I am stumped.' His eyes held hers. 'Quite mystified.'

'It's Melandra.'

'Ah—Melandra.' He drew in air between his teeth. 'It sounds like a Latin name—is that possible?'

'I only know that it's a very old name in my family which cropped up again when I was christened.'

'Interesting.' His eyes swept her from head to foot, decidedly a look which made her catch at the door handle. She was halfway out of the door when he called after her:

'I shall be seeing you, Melandra.'

The threat and promise mingling in his voice sent Melly hurrying away from his room, almost forgetting in her haste to take the lunch trolley with her. Though twenty-two years old, Melly was a girl who kept a distance between herself and men . . . and never in her life before had she met a man who magnetised her thoughts for hours after her encounter with him.

Determined to stay out of his disturbing orbit, she switched rounds with one of the other girls who served meals to the patients. She strove not to enquire about his progress, though she was naturally curious. She felt sure that he'd soon be back on his feet and causing havoc with the hearts of other women he came into contact with.

For some reason there was a free and rather
ruthless air about Jourdan Lanier that suggested
the bachelor rather than the married man.

In the days that followed Melly kept herself
busy and had almost put the Frenchman out of
her thoughts when he casually walked back into
them. On the day of his discharge from the clinic
he appeared in the kitchen where Melly was
peeling vegetables, and dismayed as she was to
see him she couldn't help noticing how striking
he looked in a smooth brown suit worn with a
cream-toned shirt and brown tie, a tailored
trench coat slung around his shoulders like a
cloak.

Upright and out of his sickbed he compelled
Melly's attention more than ever, seizing and
holding her gaze for a long moment as he stood
there.

'I have been ordered to convalesce for a few
weeks,' he informed her, frowning as he swung
his glance round the kitchen with its cooking
stoves and saucepans and piles of crockery.
'When I return to London I should like you to
have dinner with me. You will come?'

Melly gazed at him speechlessly. Further
involvement with this man was out of the
question and she had to be firm about it . . . with
herself as much as with him. Probably he was
only being polite and wanted to show his
gratitude because she had been his Samaritan,
but even so it wouldn't be wise of her to say yes
to him. She was about to refuse his invitation
when he spoke again:

'You will come.' This time it was a statement
rather than a query. 'I shall be in touch with you,
Melandra.'

He walked away and left her standing there with a bunch of carrots in her hand, and later on, to her further dismay, large bouquets of flowers began to arrive at her tiny flat in one of the tall old houses off the Marylebone Road. Gorgeous blooms, always with a small card attached bearing evocative little messages.

Quotations such as: *Trifles console us because trifles disturb us. By flight we often run into our fate.*

There was never a name on the cards, but Melly received the message, and a quotation leapt into her mind. *Beware of people bearing gifts.*

Lacking space for all the flowers, she took some of them to the clinic and placed them in the rooms of patients who had none. The gesture was put down to her own generosity; she didn't dare confide in anyone, too secretly scared and excited to be able to discuss Jourdan Lanier in the casual way the nurses discussed their male friends with each other.

And when her inquisitive landlady expressed the view that her 'boy-friend' must have money in order to send her such expensive flowers, Melly firmly told her that he was a grateful patient and that was all.

Boy-friend, indeed! One look at Jourdan Lanier had informed Melly that he had been the sort of youth who had matured rapidly, and she was also aware that several of the nurses had hoped for a closer relationship with him.

Melly wondered if by staying out of his room at the clinic she had aroused not only his curiosity about her, but his instinct to pursue a girl who chose to elude him.

A rather anxious look began to show in her

eyes, which had a slightly triangular shape in her face whose bones were clearly defined beneath her smooth skin. The colour of her eyes was a deep, clear honey, with a friendly expression veiled by a touch of reserve. Melly was a girl who would instinctively help anyone, but at the same time she never established close relationships with those she came into contact with. A barrier was there and a little warning light in the honey-gold eyes indicated that she was a private person who intended to stay that way.

Melly had been reared by her grandmother, a God-fearing and resilient Devonshire woman who had taken the young Melandra into her care and keeping when Melly's father, a widower, chose to go and work abroad. He sent home money so Melly could be well cared for, then one day a telegram arrived, briefly explaining that he'd been killed in a car accident.

Melly had felt saddened, but she hadn't really known him and her young life revolved around her grandmother, there in the village of Bryde in the tawny thatched cottage along Rebel Lane. Always there were flowers in the garden, honeysuckle and pansies, granny-bonnets and stocks, foxgloves and her great favourite, the marigold. In winter a shroud of snow would cover the fields and hedgerows and with other children of the village she would roll snow until the ball grew awesomely large.

Leaving school at sixteen, Melly had gone to work at a local riding-school, for like other children of the locality she grew up fearless of the moorland ponies and loved to ride them. It was only later that she came to work in London.

Darling Gran, she would have advised Melly to

forget such a man as Jourdan Lanier, had she still been there at Bryde to write to and visit.

Melly told herself that if Jourdan Lanier was intrigued because some of her blood ran in his veins and it had given him ideas of an intimate nature, then he was in for a disappointment. She was adamant about that.

It was on a Friday evening when Melly's landlady came knocking on her door to tell her that she was wanted on the telephone, which was down in the hall.

'Sounds like a foreign gentleman, dear.' The woman's eyes were agleam with curiosity, for during the months Melly had been one of her tenants she had never been known to encourage the attentions of men, least of all a man who sent her expensive bunches of flowers.

'Could you tell him I'm not at home?' Melly was grilling a chop for her supper. 'My meal will get cold, a-and I don't really want to speak to him.'

'Don't be such a silly girl.' Her landlady switched off the grill. 'You go and find out what he wants—run along with you!'

Biting her lip with nervousness, Melly walked down the stairs as slowly as possible and approached the telephone as if it were a snake hanging on the wall, ready to throw its coils around her. 'Hello?' she said, in a reluctant tone of voice.

'Melandra?' The deep masculine voice was unmistakable.

'Yes.' Melly ran the tip of her tongue around dry lips.

'I said I would be in touch, remember? You received my flowers?'

'It was kind of you to send them, but——'

'Did you like them?'

'Of course, but you shouldn't spend your money on a stranger.'

'I don't consider us to be strangers,' he replied. 'I'm walking around and breathing the good air because of you.'

'Oh, they'd have found you another donor, Mr Lanier.'

'Ours is a rare blood group, child, and I had a burst appendix.'

'I know—are you feeling rested after your holiday?'

'I feel extremely fit again. How are you, Melandra?'

'Oh, I've been keeping busy, thank you. It really was kind of you to send me the flowers and they're really lovely—my sitting-room looks like a conservatory.'

'I didn't want you to forget me.'

'Oh, as if I could——' Melly broke off, staring at the wall in consternation. 'What I mean is— you know, being the one who was able to be of help——'

'You felt involved, eh?'

'Yes, I'd have been very downcast had the transfusion not been of any use to you.'

'I should have been even more downcast, Melandra.' He spoke drily. 'So you will come and have dinner with me tomorrow evening?'

Her heart leapt . . . oh, how she longed to say yes, and how hard it was to say no. 'I—I usually go to the cinema on Saturday evenings.'

'Then it will make a change for you to dine at the Ritz.'

'You mean *the* Ritz?'

'If you don't fancy the Ritz we can go to McDonald's, take your choice.'

She knew he was joking about McDonald's but not about that other far more glamorous place. 'It's kind of you to ask me, Mr Lanier, but I can't possibly accept——'

'Stop being so exasperating, young woman!' Suddenly there was a forceful note in his voice. 'Stop this dilly-dallying.'

'I—I'm going to the cinema with someone.' Melly was getting desperate. 'I've got a date.'

'Then I suggest you break it, though my information is that you don't go out with young men.'

'Who's been talking to you about me?' She felt a stab of alarm.

'I have my sources, Melandra.'

'By the name of Nurse Rosie Wing, by any chance?' Rosie was a Chinese nurse at the clinic with whom Melly was friendly and she had been one of the nurses in charge of Jourdan Lanier.

'Yes, that is the name,' he admitted. 'Tell me, what is it about me that makes you afraid?'

'I—I'm not afraid of you,' she denied.

'Then prove it—say you will have dinner with me at the Ritz.'

'I really don't know why you're so persistent, Mr Lanier,' Melly sighed.

'Come now, you are being coy.'

'Rosie Wing is much prettier than I am, so why not ask her to go out with you?'

'Rosie is a delightful person, but I happen to be interested in you.'

'There isn't a lot about me to interest you, Mr Lanier.'

'There I disagree. Too many women are so

obvious and it's in my nature to like a mystery.' He paused to let her absorb his remark. 'I shall call for you around seven-thirty tomorrow evening.'

'No—please!' Her fingers clenched the telephone cord.

'That is a contradiction that intrigues me.' He laughed briefly and Melly had a vision of his hard white teeth. 'I don't take no for an answer.'

'Least of all from a woman?' she interposed.

'Exactly. Come, you have to admit that after all my pain and suffering I need to celebrate the fact that I am back among the living. I want you to celebrate with me.'

'London is full of girls who want to enjoy themselves on Saturday evening.' Melly had to try and convince him that she was quite content to spend her evening alone at the cinema.

'Yes, all shapes, sizes and colours,' he agreed, 'and quite a few of them only too willing to please a man. It's perverse of me to seek your company, is it not?'

'Perhaps you're tired of the easy conquest, Mr Lanier.'

'My name is Jourdan.'

'And I bet even your closest friends don't call you Jordy.'

'They wouldn't dare.'

'Which is why I'm not coming out with you, Mr Lanier, because you like your own way.'

'Don't most men?'

'I expect so.'

'You don't sound too sure,' he observed.

'I've never been a girl to run around with every joker in the pack,' said Melly primly.

'And that again is why I'm asking you to have

dinner with me. Have you ever tasted pink champagne?'

'No.'

'Who taught you to be wary of men and their intentions?'

'Instinct.'

'And is your instinct telling you that I am out to get all I can from you, Melly?'

'You're a man,' she replied, and wasn't likely to forget the way he had looked in bed, with his bare brown chest and those whipcord arms that looked as if once they were around a girl she'd have a struggle to get out of them.

'Yes, I'm a man,' his voice mocked her, 'and I consider that nature planned it rather well, making a man so opposite to a girl.'

'And it's the girl who pays when the fun is over, Mr Lanier.'

'You seem to have got it into your head, young woman, that I'm planning to seduce you. Do you consider yourself so irresistible?'

'No——' She blushed. 'Of course I don't.'

'Then why are you trying to put me off? All I'm suggesting is that we dine together, and I do assure you that I don't expect to be rewarded—not if the young lady's reluctant.'

Her blush deepened, then before she could plunge into any more excuses that got her nowhere, he said decisively: 'Be ready on time, I don't care to be kept waiting.'

There was a click and then a purring sound that indicated he had rung off. Melly hung up the receiver and as she walked upstairs her knees felt trembly and tiny wings seemed to be fluttering in the centre of her stomach. She felt oddly excited and breathless, and decided that a cup of tea might help to calm her down.

As she set the kettle to boil and placed a teabag in her teapot she had visions of the Ritz Restaurant. A place that spelled glamour, with waiters bringing delicious food to a table she shared with a very worldly Latin. He had been quite ill following his operation and it somehow made a refusal to dine with him very ungracious.

There came a scratching on her door, and teacup in hand, she opened it and in strolled Podge, her landlady's fluffy white cat. 'Hello, boy,' she smiled, 'I suppose you've come scrounging for some supper.'

He gazed up at her and blinked his golden eyes, too beguiling for Melly to resist, and she wasn't really hungry any more. She cut her cold chop into pieces and put the plate down for Podge, who tucked in with relish.

Melly sat down and sipped her cup of tea, nibbling idly at a biscuit while her resolve not to go out with Jourdan Lanier gradually melted away until she began to ponder on what she should wear to go dining at the Ritz. She had some money saved and could afford to buy a nice dress, and with a growing sense of expectation she watched the contented Podge rubbing his big paw back and forth among his whiskers.

Cats were easier to please than people, she reflected. All they asked of life was a nice piece of fish, a mouse to chase, and a corner where they could curl up and sleep. A person didn't have to be on guard with them, but it was different with someone like Jourdan Lanier, who was so forcefully attractive ... so very different from anyone else she had ever known.

Yes, she admitted to herself, she wanted to
swish into the Ritz at the side of such a man, and
she wanted to taste pink champagne and live on
the memory of such an evening for a long time
afterwards.

CHAPTER ONE

MELLY felt shy and tongue-tied driving through the West End in a black cab, wearing a dress that felt like a silky skin in a shade the shop assistant had called topaz. There hadn't been much she could do about her straight fair hair except wash and comb it until it shone like a bell about her head, and in her earlobes she wore the tiny tiger-eyes which had belonged to her grandmother.

Jourdan Lanier sat watching her from his corner of the cab, his grey eyes shaded by lashes that matched his hair. Her pulses stirred at the sight of him, for he looked very distinguished in a dinner jacket and a ruffled white shirt with a green stone glinting in it.

'You are pleasing to look at, Melandra.' His voice rose from the depths of the brown throat behind the hand-tied tie and the Edwardian pin.

'Thank you, Mr Lanier.' She sat there with an outward air of composure, hands folded around her beaded purse.

'Won't you make the effort to call me Jourdan?' he asked, with a touch of amusement. 'It isn't such a bad name, is it?'

'It's a very nice name.' She felt a flow of warmth at the way his eyes travelled over her; the worldly eyes of a man who knew a lot about women. 'I'm gratified that you made up your mind to have dinner with me.'

'It will make a change from fish and chips,' she replied, lips denting in a smile. 'That's what I usually take home for my supper when I come out of the cinema.'

His eyes glinted there beyond the shadow of his lashes. 'You have a certain candour as well as a touch of mystery.'

'I was brought up to be truthful, so I try to be.'

'Then be honest and admit that my company is not displeasing you.'

'How could I be displeased with a man who is going to treat me to a delicious dinner, Mr Lanier?'

'I am called Jourdan.' He leaned towards her so suddenly that she drew back in alarm. He seemed to enjoy her alarm, a hand reaching to her chin and gripping it. 'Say my name—and that's an order!'

'Why should I take orders from you?' she protested, her wide golden eyes fixed upon his dark face. 'You probably expect obedience from your French girls, but I don't happen to be one of them!'

'On the contrary, you are behaving as if I must be kept at arm's length because your precious virtue is at stake.' But even as he spoke his hand slid to her neck and his hard fingers encircled its slim bareness. 'I can feel your pulse, Melandra, hammering away beneath my fingertips. You really are afraid of me, aren't you?'

'I—I'm a little nervous,' she confessed. 'I've never dined at the Ritz and I know it's a very smart place.'

'So that is the reason for the racing pulse—and I was thinking it was my fatal attraction!' His hand slid to her silken shoulder and instantly she tensed.

'Don't do that!' She shrugged away from him.

His eyes narrowed and he leaned back into his corner. 'You act like a girl who has been frightened by someone?'

'I—I don't want you to get the wrong idea about me, Mr Lanier. I don't happen to be free with my favours—call me old-fashioned.'

'So you are not the type of English blonde it is risky for a man to share a cab with?'

'Oh, you're quite safe with me.' Her sense of humour returned now he had been put at arm's length. 'Foreign men shouldn't believe all they read about English girls—we are as mixed as the flowers in a cottage garden and sometimes there are nettles among the daisies.'

'So I am about to share the evening with a stinging nettle, eh?'

'I won't sting, Mr Lanier, if you promise not to touch.'

He inclined his dark head and his smile was a fleeting glimmer of strong white teeth. 'As I suspected, there is a spine of steel in your girlish frame, and I think you learned good things from your grandmother, eh?'

'I did,' she said warmly. 'She was moral without being rigid, and I was with her from a small child.'

'Good lessons learned early are the best ones.' His eyes dwelt steadily upon her face. 'I, too, had a little black-clad grandmother who used to make lace and talk to me of the folk-heroes of France. We, much like the British, have a long history interwoven with romantic heroes such as Lancelot of the Lake. It would be a shame if young people lost their belief in the powers of romance, eh?'

'I'm glad you understand,' she smiled, 'and don't think me a prig.'

'No, you have standards which I accept and respect, believe me.'

'Do you truly—believe?'

'Cross my heart, for was it not a touch of fate that you were working at the clinic when I needed you? Are you registered as a blood donor?'

'No——' She bit her lip. 'I'm listed as a stand-by donor because of belonging to the Tj (a) negative blood group.'

'So it was very fortunate for me that you were on duty at the clinic when I was rushed in—it teaches a man not to go around with a pain in the hope that it will go away.' He grimaced, as if at the memory of his pain. 'I have relatives in London, you see. My brother is at the Embassy and his wife had planned a dinner to which I was invited and I didn't wish to disappoint her—we had reached the meat course when I suddenly became ill. The next thing I knew was that I awakened in a sickroom and there was a nurse checking my pulse.'

As he spoke he reached for Melly's hand and studied the work-worn look of her slender fingers. His fingers were strong and brown and there was a carved ring on the middle finger of the hand that held hers. The cuffs at his wrists looked fiercely white against his skin, into which the sun of France had probably burned itself.

'Tell me why you work in a hospital kitchen, Melandra.'

'Because I like it.' Her pulse was hammering and her fingers felt helplessly locked within his grasp.

'Why not be a nurse if you like caring for the sick?'

'Oh, you have to start training quite early and I—I didn't come to London until I was twenty.'

'I see. And what did you do for your living before you came to the city?'

'I worked at a riding-school.' Her fingers struggled for their release. 'I don't mind my work at the clinic. I do my job quite happily, Mr Lanier.'

'I'm insisting that you call me by my first name. We shouldn't stand on ceremony, you and I. We are connected by blood, remember.'

'I'll try——'

'And succeed before the evening is over.' And as he spoke he carried her hand to his lips and kissed it. A minute later, to her relief, the cab drew into the curb at the hotel entrance of the Ritz, where a uniformed doorman opened the cab door for them to descend to the pavement.

Their arrival had saved Melly from having to snatch her hand from those lips which had felt so warm and sensual against her skin.

'Good evening, madam. Good evening, sir.' The doorman accepted his tip and ushered them through the swing doors where a rose-coloured carpet led along a Regency furnished colonnade.

For Melly the ambience of the Ritz lived up to her every expectation. Everything was so glamorous and dreamlike, the very air permeated by a tang of perfume, wine and coffee.

There were glazed display cabinets in which jewellery and charming items of bric-à-brac were set out, and overhead from a gilded ceiling hung chandeliers like jewels, glittering upon the cherubs that adorned the columns and the mirrors. Elegant chairs were set in front of

Regency writing-tables, and couches matched the cream and rose décor.

It was like stepping back into a more gracious time, Melly thought to herself, and the waiters should have been wearing satin breeches and powdered wigs.

At the side of Jourdan Lanier she mounted a wide curve of marble steps to the cocktail lounge where a secluded table had been reserved for them. There were little bowls of nuts and crackers on the table, and in a cooler stood their bottle of champagne, from which the cork was withdrawn with a hiss and a pop. Melly watched as their glasses were filled by the waiter, and she broke into a smile when she saw that the champagne really was pink.

'Does the *signorina* celebrate her birthday, sir?' The waiter glanced at Melly with knowing Italian eyes; he could see that this was her first visit to the Ritz.

'*Non*, we are just celebrating.' Grey eyes looked across into Melly's and she told herself that he had managed to make those words sound suggestive, and she didn't miss the way the waiter glanced at her left hand as if expecting to see a brand new ring sparkling there.

'We'll enjoy our champagne, Enrico, before taking a look at the menu.'

'*Si*.' The waiter gave a courteous inclination of his head and left them together.

Jourdan raised his glass, and Melly did the same. 'I salute youth,' he said. 'It sparkles like champagne and then before we realise it the bubbles have dwindled. Thank you, Melly, for being on hand when I needed you.'

'You're welcome, sir.'

'Melly,' he looked threatening, 'do I have to wring my name from your lips, you obstinate child?'

'Just give me time to—to get used to you.' She took a questing sip of her pink champagne. 'Mmmm, this is delicious. I could get to like this!'

Amusedly he watched her, looking very worldly and at home in the stylish surroundings of the Ritz. 'I can think of several other things you should get to like.'

She refused to answer him and gazed around her with wide-eyed interest. 'Buckingham Palace can't be grander than this place—how amazed my dear Gran would be if she could see me now!'

'Perhaps she can, *petite*.' Jourdan raised his wine glass to his lips, his eyes frankly appraising Melly in the topaz-coloured dress, styled along simple lines befitting her slim-hipped figure. 'It is a nice thought that those we have been close to are watching over us, eh?'

'I hope it's true,' Melly murmured. 'I—I often feel that Gran is near me and still caring about me. But I——' She broke off and sipped some more champagne.

'You were about to say something?'

'Oh, it was nothing—just a thought.'

'Please share the thought with me.'

'It surprises me, that you believe there might be an afterlife.'

'Did you take me for a total cynic, young woman?'

'You seem very sophisticated to me,' she explained.

'Compared to you, Melly, I am very sophisticated, but that doesn't mean that I have lost all my faith in the ideals of youth.' His smile when it came held a slight touch of melancholy. 'You are a disarmingly unpretentious young person, do you know that, Melly?'

'I do now you've told me.' She wasn't unaware that other women in the cocktail lounge were looking at Jourdan with speculation in their eyes. He wasn't easy to assess. He could have been a gentleman of leisure, a tycoon out on the town, even an actor, with his strongly defined face.

It was exciting, she realised, being aware of the real truth. Knowing that this strong and attractive man was enjoying life again because of her.

Grown shy of his eyes, Melly fixed her gaze upon the dent in his chin. 'Did you go to Nice or St Tropez to convalesce?' she asked. 'You're very tanned—you make all the other men in this lounge look insipid.'

'You shouldn't be looking at other men,' he reproved. 'You don't see me looking at other women, do you?'

'All the same, you're aware of them, aren't you? I don't think a Frenchman misses much where women are concerned.'

He merely smiled and took a leather case from an inside pocket of his dinner jacket. 'Do you mind if I smoke? I'd offer you one of these if my Latin instincts didn't tell me that you number non-smoking among your virtues.'

'I'm not a prig,' she objected, watching as he fired the tip of his cheroot. 'Where did you go to get such a tan?'

'To Bel-Aze, an island in the Caribbean. I have a house there—ah, you look amazed. Why is that?'

'Because you don't look the domesticated type. Is it a nice house?'

'I think so. It has big open verandas and is very secluded—I got tanned all over.'

There was a wicked gleam in his eyes as they roved Melly's face. 'You look as if you could do with a holiday, young woman. When was the last time you had one?'

'Last August.' Her mind shied away from the image he had induced of himself, lazing on a sunlit beach after a swim in jewel-blue waters . . . it was tempting, as well as tormenting, to imagine herself beside him on that beach. 'I went home to Devon for a week, but it made me rather sad, seeing Gran's cottage in other hands. A lot of her cottage garden flowers were gone and there were painted gnomes in their place——'

Melly broke off with a choke in her voice. 'Everything changes when we grow up, doesn't it?'

'Inevitably, *ma petite*, but not always for the worst. You are at the best time of your life and you should be having fun.' Jourdan spoke with almost a touch of anger. 'You need taking in hand, and I've a good mind to do it!'

'You wouldn't get very far,' she retorted. 'My life is the way I want it——'

'You don't mean what you say, Melly.' He gestured with his cheroot. 'Look around you and you will see women with only half your charm and youth and they are making sure they have a good time.'

'There's more to life than having a good time,' she argued.

'There is more to life than just working and going home to a lonely pair of rooms and

watching a movie on Saturday nights. You have
got to come out of your shell before it gets so
attached to you that you will feel insecure unless
you are tucked inside it.' He regarded her
through the twining smoke of his cheroot, his
grey eyes narrowed. 'What has made you this
way—those warm-sherry eyes should always be
laughing?'

Melly felt herself flushing at his compliment
about her eyes. 'I—I agreed to dine with you, Mr
Lanier, but I didn't say I'd tell you the story of
my life.'

'*Mon Dieu!*' He swung his fingers as if burned.
'You can be quite blistering when you like—shall
I make a guess about you? You fell for a young
man and he let you down, so you decided to cut
love and romance out of your life. Am I correct?'

'No, you're way off the mark.' Reserve veiled
her eyes, for Jourdan Lanier was the last person
she could confide in. As she looked at him, the
light of the brilliant chandeliers in his dark hair,
his skin so deeply tanned against the crisp
whiteness of his shirt, he thrust his way through
the guard she kept on her inmost feelings and she
just had to be on the defensive with him.

'I see.' He tapped ash into a tray. 'You are
really a runaway nun, eh?'

He meant her to laugh and she did so. 'Don't
let's talk about me any more; I've led a very
ordinary life. How did you come to own a house
on a tropical island—oh, you're married, of
course!'

'I am divorced.' He said it quite casually,
almost dismissively, as if he were brushing ash
from his sleeve. 'I have a young daughter from
the marriage who lives in America with her

mother. I should like to see more of her, but until recently it couldn't always be managed. So now, Melly, we know a little more about each other. You are a single girl who is shy of men, and I have a child from a marriage which failed.'

As he finished speaking the waiter came to refill their glasses. 'Are you ready to order, sir?' he asked.

'We might as well, Enrico.'

Menu cards were handed to them and after a moment Jourdan asked her if she fancied caviar to start with.

'Do you mean it?' Her eyes lit up. 'I've always wondered what it tastes like.'

'You will find it intriguing. Now what about your main choice? Dover sole, fillet steak, or perhaps roast pork and trimmings?'

'Roast pork, please.' She spoke hungrily, remembering the cold chop of last night which the cat had eaten.

The tanned cheek clefted and as he ordered their meal, Melly took a luxurious sip of her champagne and idly wondered what her escort really thought of her, a girl so obviously unused to dining in the company of a man, especially one so worldly as himself. A thought which led her on to wonder what kind of a woman his wife had been? Soignée and self-engrossed like some of those women who entered the clinic to have their youth renewed by cosmetic surgery? It had become a fad with so many women, so intent on preserving their outer image that they forgot to care about their inner selves, such as having a warm and loving heart.

'Do you mind my country voice?' she suddenly asked Jourdan.

'No, I find it rather refreshing.' He quirked an eyebrow. 'Should I mind it, Melly?'

'Some people think that country girls are unworldly.'

'Have you a yearning to be sophisticated?' His eyes dwelt glintingly on her face, with the clear skin that was obviously due to her upbringing in the fresh, unpolluted air of the Devon countryside. Allied to her wide, enquiring eyes she did look unspoilt.

'I expect you're used to worldly women,' she remarked, her fingers at play upon the stem of her wine glass, a little sign that she was nervous of his gaze.

'Do you take all Frenchmen for rakes?' he asked quizzically. 'It might surprise you to learn that my grandmother was Welsh and my grandfather a man who worked down in the coalmines—an aspect of my background which never suited my wife Irene.' The waiter came to confer about wine with their dinner, and Melly realised that Jourdan had been married to one of those rather artificial women who only seemed alive when they were impressing people with their looks and lineage and style of dress. The kind of women who loved themselves far more than they ever loved anyone else.

'Are you feeling ravenous?' Jourdan had suddenly leaned across the table and captured her eyes. 'You have that kind of faraway look—or are you dreaming of an island in the sun?'

'No—I'm dying for my dinner!' Melly gave him a confused look. 'I only had a toasted teacake for my lunch because I had to go and buy this dress. The girl in the shop said it was my colour, but I—I spent rather more than I intended.'

'I'm flattered that you should do so, Melly.'
His gaze slid over her slim figure. 'The dress is
very fetching and it suits you.'

'I was staggered by the price.' Melly bit her
lip; she seemed to be harping on money, but the
dress had taken a large bite out of her small hoard
of savings. 'I don't want to sound like a
miser——'

'I quite understand your dilemma.' His eyes
pierced like steel through his black lashes. 'Your
job at the clinic is probably underpaid.'

'But I like working there, Mr—Jourdan.'

'Champagne, quickly.' He mockingly raised his
glass. 'You called me by my name!'

'Don't take the mickey out of me,' she said
defensively.

'The mickey?' He quirked an eyebrow. 'You
think I taunt you, eh?'

'I know you think I'm naïve——'

'You don't know at all what I think, and now
it's time to go in to dinner.' He pushed back his
chair and came round to Melly's side and taking
her by the hand raised her to her feet. They
crossed to the wide steps that led down to the
colonnade and Melly could see their two figures
reflected in the long mirrors . . . the girl in the
ale-coloured silk was herself, and the tall man was
a disturbing stranger who had entered her life for
a brief while and whom she wouldn't see again
after tonight.

They were led to a table set with lamps and
flowers, and when Melly sat down the waiter
shook out the crisp napkin and spread it on her
lap. 'Thank you,' she smiled, and could feel her
heart beating fast with the pleasure of the
moment.

She glanced around the gracious dining-room where very often the famous and newsworthy came to enjoy the glamorous surroundings and the expensive food.

'I can see you aren't disappointed,' Jourdan remarked. 'Your eyes tell their own story.'

'Do I seem terribly naïve?' she asked.

'I think you are very natural,' he replied. 'A hard-working young woman who does not assume that the moon and the stars should be hers for the asking.' He held her gaze across the table as if searching her eyes for something that eluded him. 'You seem uncomplicated, but I don't think you are—you have depths, Melandra.'

'Do you come here often?' she asked quickly, for he seemed at home in this grand place where he called the waiters by their names.

'Whenever I come to London, and when I have a companion I would like to impress.'

'Now you're flattering me,' she said, without a tinge of coyness. Melly had been taught by her grandmother to be forthright, and also she was determined not to be swept away by the charm of Jourdan Lanier.

'Don't you like to be flattered by a man?' A smile moved through his eyes. 'Most women lap it up as if it were cream; they can't get enough of it.'

'I don't mind, if it's sincere and isn't just part of the—game.'

'And what game is that, Melly?'

'You know very well what game I'm referring to.'

'You obviously think that I play it a lot and have now reached Olympic standards.'

She broke into a smile. 'If you Frenchmen will insist on being labelled as the world's best lovers, then you can't blame a country girl like me from assuming it to be true!'

'Don't forget my dash of Welsh blood—perhaps it dilutes my French tendencies.' He snapped a breadstick with his firm teeth. 'Do you take me for a playboy?'

'I—I don't know——' It came to Melly that she really knew very little about him. 'Are you in the Diplomatic Service like your brother?'

'You could say that, except that I am in a service which in your country is called the S.A.S.'

Melly caught her breath, then realised that on first seeing Jourdan she had looked upon the taut, trained body of a fighting man. That from their first encounter there had been something about him that suggested the daring Crusader.

'I see.' She smiled tentatively. 'You do a dangerous job, so why shouldn't you have fun when you're on leave?'

'You can indeed say, Melly, that after months in the company of men it feels good to be with a girl. It makes quite a change to look at smooth skin and to smell perfume after the tang of uniforms.'

'But I bet you don't often date the kitchen help.' She didn't know why she said it, but whenever he said something personal Melly felt herself getting panicky. Instinct had warned her that it wasn't possible to be in the company of such a man without feeling drawn to him, and she couldn't allow such a thing to happen.

'Do you know,' a dangerous glint had come into his eyes, 'you could do with a good spanking!

You are here with me tonight solely for the reason that I wanted you here. Now relax and stop being on the defensive all the time—you make me feel that I am back on active service!'

'When do you go back?' she asked.

'Are you so eager to be rid of me?'

'N-no——'

'I am on extended leave at present. I want to go and see my daughter and I'm hoping to spend a little time with her.'

He withdrew into his thoughts and Melly wondered what his little girl was like. Did she resemble his wife or himself? Probably she resembled Jourdan as he was so dominant in personality and looks.

'As a matter of fact,' he said at last, 'I have almost made up my mind to leave the service. A man begins to feel the urge to settle down and I am well past thirty. I want to see more of Jody. She's starting to grow up and if I don't take care she will suddenly be an adult and we shan't know each other.'

'How old is she?' Melly liked to hear him confiding in her, but still she kept a guard on her feelings. She firmly told herself that he told her these things because she had a sympathetic manner, and though he looked so well he had suffered that lowering of the spirits which an operation leaves in its wake.

'She was twelve last December.' A smile edged his mouth. 'She is getting taller, starting to be a big girl, and Irene isn't keen about that. Irene has a phobia about growing old, so she spends a lot of her time preserving her precious face and figure, but when people see her with Jody they realise that Irene is no spring chicken. I have the feeling

she would not fight me too hard if I wanted
custody of Jody, but I need to offer the child a
proper home and my house at Bel-Aze is a
bachelor establishment at the present time.'

The waiter came and served their caviar, along
with thin slices of brown bread, balls of butter
and wedges of lemon. After squeezing on the
lemon juice Melly tasted the caviar and found it
delicious.

'Now you are having fun, eh?' Jourdan smiled
across into her eyes.

Melly smiled back spontaneously and found
herself wondering how his wife could possibly let
him go out of her life. She savoured another
mouthful of caviar and took a sip of wine. 'You
believe in living well when you're on leave, don't
you?'

'Just as I believe in dying well.' He raised his
wine glass. 'But that chapter is over and another
is beginning ... let us hope that when I need
another favour of you, Melly, you will agree to
grant it. Do you think you might?'

She gave him a faintly suspicious look and he
laughed quietly as he caught it. 'Not that kind of
favour, Miss Touch-me-not!'

CHAPTER THREE

MELLY chose orange chiffon pie for dessert, and it was so heavenly that she informed Jourdan she would probably dream about it.

'What a blow to my ego!' He placed a piece of Camembert cheese on a wedge of biscuit. 'So you would sooner dream about a piece of pie than about me?'

'Oh, you've got plenty of women to dream about you.' She placed another spoonful of the delicious pie in her mouth and wondered how it was made . . . not that there was much chance of cooking something so delicious on a two-ringed gas cooker.

'You have me labelled as a real lady-chaser, haven't you, Melly? What have I done to make you think of me in such a way?'

'Well, you're *macho*, as they say in the movies.'

'If you mean I have muscles, admittedly I have them, but that doesn't mean that I am always exercising them in some lady's bed. Many of the real Casanovas are men who seem outwardly timid—don't you know that you can't judge a pie from the crust on top?'

Melly gave him a startled look. 'My grandmother used to say that!'

'And so did mine, young woman. Don't forget my Welsh grandmother. I have valley lore and honour in me and don't you forget it.'

'I'm sorry,' she said contritely. 'But most of the nurses at the clinic were mooning over you,

and they know far more about men than I do. I
mean, they go out on dates and get involved with
men, but I—I steer clear of all that.'

'I am curious to know why, Melly. You are
here with me, so you can't be altogether a man-
hater. You certainly don't look like one, not with
those eyes of yours and those soft young lips.'

'Please don't say such things—I don't want to
hear them!'

'What would you prefer me to say, that you put
my teeth on edge?' He studied her intently.
'Come, be frank with me, are you planning to
take very devout vows that make it a sin for a
man to say pleasing things to you?'

'Of course not——'

'You might as well, *petite*. If you are going to
keep men at arm's length, you had certainly
better cover your hair and not wear silk against
that creamy skin. Join an enclosed order where
anything male is strictly taboo.'

Melly finished her pie and dabbed her lips with
her napkin. Jourdan looked really annoyed with
her, but she had to let it be that way. She
couldn't respond to his overtures and allow this
evening to drift towards any kind of intimacy.
She had to let him believe that she was frigid.

'Coffee?' He regarded her with a frown.

'Please.'

'You have enjoyed your dinner?'

'Every mouthful, thank you.'

'I am glad something has pleased you—it
would seem that I don't!'

She made no protest. He mustn't be allowed to
know that in his well-cut evening suit she
thought him the most attractive man in the room.
She must hide her true feelings from him.

'I should not have persisted in asking you to come out with me,' he said. 'Obviously you had reservations, and after we've had our coffee I shall take you home.'

'I could go by underground to save you the bother——'

'*Mon Dieu*,' he glowered at her through his lashes, 'what a little man-hater you are! I shall return you to your lodgings just to make sure you get there, but rest assured that I won't lay a finger on you. I should be afraid it might drop off with frostbite!'

They were drinking their coffee when a hand with silvered fingernails touched Jourdan on the shoulder. 'Hello, stranger! I was certain it was you even though you had your back to me ... there's something, darling, about the way you hold your head.'

Melly glanced up at the woman who was gazing down at Jourdan, and because she had a good memory for faces she instantly recognized the elegantly dressed woman as a patient who had been discharged from the clinic a few weeks ago. She had been in to have her eyelids lifted, and to have a breast implant corrected. Right now she was looking svelte and pleased with herself, though her behaviour as a patient had been less than charming.

'Caroline!' Jourdan stood up and taking her by the hand brushed his lips across the back of it. 'How good to see you.'

'Ditto, darling. Now tell me, what have you been doing with yourself—you look thinner.' She touched his face with a silver-tinted hand and the gesture was seductive. 'I did hear a rumour that you were under the weather—true or false?'

'I did spend a few days in hospital, but it was nothing too serious. How are you, Caroline? You are looking very chic.'

'I'm feeling my oats, darling.' She fluttered her lashes at him as her gaze slid to Melly, who sensed right away that her age was being calculated along with the cost of her dress.

'I feel sure we've met,' the woman remarked, 'but I can't for the moment place you. Was it at the Courtenay girl's engagement party?'

Melly felt a stab of amusement and shook her head. It wouldn't be quite fair in front of Jourdan to reveal the fact that during Caroline's stay at the clinic she had been served her meals from Melly's trolley.

'Melly, meet a friend of mine.' Jourdan shared his quizzical smile between them. 'Mrs Caroline Frome.'

'How do you do, Mrs Frome?' When Melly spoke there was no concealing the fact that she wasn't from Belgrave Square or adjacent areas, and Caroline Frome narrowed her eyes in concentration.

'Good heavens——!'

'What is it, Caroline?' Jourdan regarded her with a gleam of amusement in his eyes. 'Did you forget something?'

'Oh—not a thing. So, poor pet, you've been laid on your back in hospital—may one enquire the cause, for you've always looked as fit as a fiddle? Quaint saying, isn't it?'

'Quaint,' he agreed, and glanced at Melly. 'Is it one of those country village sayings? I'm sure you would know.'

'My grandmother would have known.' Melly could feel herself getting tense, for it seemed as if

Jourdan was amusing himself at her expense; annoyed with her, she supposed, for not giving him the kind of look he was enjoying from his friend Caroline.

A look that changed rapidly when the woman glanced again at Melly ... abruptly there was recognition in her eyes and it became evident that she was snobbishly curious to know what Jourdan Lanier was doing in the company of a girl she had regarded as a servant. At the clinic she had treated Melly as a maid of all work, there to take orders and be subservient.

Melly gazed straight back at the artificial face, and the rouged cheeks seemed to deepen in colour and the elegant body inside the silvery dress seemed to tauten, rather like a sharp sword in a sheath. The look in her eyes was deadly as they flicked the unlined, country-girl skin of Melly's face.

'Will you be going to Betty Courtenay's wedding?' she asked Jourdan. 'My sister June is to be one of her bridesmaids and you know she adores you, and she's such a vivacious girl.'

'I have been invited, being a friend of Jack Courtenay's, but I doubt if I shall attend. I'm going over to the States for a while, on a personal matter.'

'Not to get together with that stunning ex-wife of yours, Jourdan?'

'No, not to do that,' he answered in a dry tone of voice.

'What a pity, darling. Everyone thought the two of you looked so perfect together, both being such definite people.' The painted eyes found Melly, hoping she had got the point. 'Your daughter must be growing up—is she going to be as stunning as Irene?'

It was then Melly decided that she was in the way; that she was *de trop* sitting here listening to this woman stressing the fact that Jourdan Lanier's divorced wife was beautiful.

'Excuse me.' Melly pushed back her chair.

'Where are you going?' Jourdan gave her a frowning look.

'To the powder-room, darling.' Melly jumped to her feet and fled from the dining-room. The mirrored colonnade seemed endless, then at last she was pushing her way through the swing-doors into the street. The sparkling champagne bubbles had gone flat and Melly made her exit from the Ritz with her enjoyment in tatters even if her dress was still intact.

So ended Cinderella's evening with Prince Charming, she told herself, as she hurried down the steps of an adjacent subway and boarded a train that would take her part of the way home.

Her heart was thudding against her rib-bones as she sat there on the underground train, aware of a mixture of relief and distress that her evening with Jourdan Lanier was over and she was never likely to see him again. His world was far apart from hers. His kind of women were sure of themselves and casually at home in smart surroundings. Their ego, like his, had the shining surface of steel that couldn't be dented by destiny's darts.

Melly's fingers gripped her beaded purse and she gazed with unseeing eyes at the blank brick walls of the tunnels as the train surged through them, and she repeatedly told herself that she wanted never to see again that forceful, rather ironic face of the man who would no doubt end his evening in the company of Caroline Frome.

When Melly crossed the road to the bus stop she realised the lateness of the hour and the fact that few people were about in this section of the Euston Road. She gave a shiver as the night wind blew a sweet wrapper along the pavement; she had left her wrap on the back of her chair at the restaurant and the touch of chill in the air raised goosebumps on her bare arms.

'Oh, hurry up, bus!' She glanced about her, for these days it wasn't wise of a girl to be out late on her own, and now she was wishing that she had stayed at home and forgone the pink champagne. But the invitation had been flattering, not to mention the flowers with their unusual messages which she had stored away in a trinket box.

Her breath caught on a sigh. Gran used to say that what was between the covers of a mysterious book wasn't always wise reading ... a train of thought that suddenly made Melly aware that footfalls were striking the pavement behind her. It was nothing unusual to hear footsteps approaching a bus stop, but something about them raised the tiny hairs on the nape of her neck ... they were masculine and she was all alone.

Gripping her purse as if to defend herself with it, she swung round, her face strangely lit by the golden street lamps. 'Leave me alone,' she cried out. 'Don't you dare touch me!'

'Little fool!' Hands gripped and shook her. 'What a panic you are in!'

She came to her senses and found herself looking up into the face of Jourdan Lanier.

'Because you had mentioned the underground train I concluded that you had taken the subway and I knew that Baker Street station was the nearest to your lodgings. I followed on that presumption, Melly, and here you are.'

'Let me go.' She spoke quite calmly this time, the fright and panic seeping back into hiding, like the tamped-down smoke of a stirred up fire.

But still his hands held her, then suddenly he pulled her to him and bending his tall head kissed her hard upon the mouth. 'That will teach you to run out on me,' he muttered. 'I know that being kissed is something you can't tolerate.'

She tried to wrench herself out of his grip, because at last a bus was approaching. 'Take your hands off me or I'll scream blue murder and say you tried to rob me!'

'Don't talk nonsense.' He gave her a shake and looked about him, his gaze settling on a public-house whose windows were still lit, a drift of piano music stealing through its doors as a man came out into the night with a woman beside him.

'We are going over there to have a drink together,' Jourdan said firmly. 'You need one, *petite*, and I have something to say to you.'

'My bus is coming——' She tried ineffectually to escape from him. 'Stop handling me l-like a brute!'

'I have been trained not to use brutality, it only increases resistance.' And wrapping an arm of iron about her waist he propelled Melly across the road. 'Now stop behaving like a child, just because that silly creature from Belgrave Square ruffled your feathers.'

'You did some ruffling yourself!' Melly gave him a glare as he pushed her into the saloon-bar, where a smell of beer gushed around her along with the jangling piano and people talking in loud, cheerful tones.

Jourdan glanced around and saw a wedge of space at the end of the bar. 'Come along.' He urged her into the wedge, holding her there with his tall figure in the dark evening suit. Melly became aware that they were being watched, as if some of the clientele were wondering if Jourdan was a policeman.

With a sigh she leaned against the bar. It was warm in here, and she did feel shaken up and in need of the brandy which Jourdan ordered.

'It does seem to have turned a bit chilly, sir,' said the barman. 'Been to a function, you and the young lady? We don't often see evening clothes in my ale bar.'

'We have been having dinner in the West End.' Jourdan paid for the drinks. 'Have you a quieter room than this; my girl-friend is feeling slightly unwell?'

'Through there, sir.' The barman indicated an archway partly screened by a faded velvet curtain. 'That's our snuggery; you and the young lady will feel more cosy in there.'

'Excellent.' Jourdan turned to Melly, their drinks in hand. 'Let us go through, I want to talk to you.'

'I'd sooner stay in here——'

'Do as you are told, Melly.' He didn't say it in a bullying voice but with a firmness she decided to obey. They went into the snuggery, where they were given a few curious looks from the regulars in there. Jourdan indicated that Melly sit with her back to the wall so he could sit in front of her and shield her from the eyes that were looking her up and down in her silk evening dress.

She sat down resignedly. He pushed her brandy across the table and she picked up the glass and put it to her lips; his eyes willed her to drink some of it and she felt the warming glow as it went down inside her.

'I—I don't know why you bothered to follow me,' she said, keeping her voice low. 'You shouldn't have dragged yourself away from your friend Caroline.'

'She just happens to be the wife of a friend of mine, no more than that.'

'Really?' Melly forced a scoffing note into her voice. 'The two of you were getting along so well, I thought I'd leave you to your billing and cooing.'

'Jealous?' he mocked, yet with something intent in his gaze.

'Not in the least.' She looked away from him, for his grey eyes were too disturbing. 'She knew me from the clinic, if you must know, but she wasn't looking quite so glamorous the last time we met. I was serving lunch to her and she was in bed upon that occasion.'

'I wasn't aware that Caroline had been sick.' He swished the brandy in his glass. 'I do so wish you wouldn't use that hard tone of voice; it doesn't suit you.'

'Mrs Frome wasn't sick.' Melly couldn't keep a note of scorn out of her voice. 'She was in the clinic to have her eyelids lifted, not to mention some breast correction. It's bad enough when people need surgery——'

She broke off and swallowed the remainder of her brandy. 'Sorry, but that Frome woman treated me as if I was the scullerymaid. She's one of those selfish people who seem to sail through life without ever having to face something—shattering.'

'I realise it, Melly, but dismiss the idea that I admire her type of woman. Her husband is a good fellow, but men have an unfortunate knack of becoming involved with women who aren't really good for them. I am very aware of the fact!'

As he sat frowning to himself, as if reviewing his own marriage and its failure to be a happy one, piano music stole in from the other bar and Melly recognized the tune, which seemed to soothe away some of her tension.

'It's true,' Jourdan murmured, 'as time goes by the fundamental things do apply—how deeply involved are you, Melly, with your job at the clinic?'

Then without giving her time to reply, he added: 'How would you like to be my daughter's companion?'

Melly gazed at him with startled eyes. 'But your daughter lives with her mother——!'

'At present.' His features looked hard and resolved. 'But I want the child to grow up in my custody, not in Irene's. You reacted against that woman we met at the Ritz, and she's a classic example of what infatuated me before I came to my senses. There is a lot of good French blood in Jody and it would be much of a shame if it became swamped by selfish, demanding ways learned from her mother. I care deeply about that child—you must believe me, Melly.'

She searched his face and saw signs of strain there, and she pitied Jody if her mother was anything like Caroline Frome, whose devotion was entirely self-centred.

'I believe you, Jourdan. You naturally want what's best for your little girl.'

'In realising what I want, Melly, would you agree to be a companion to her?'

'I—I don't quite know what to say.' Melly could only look at him with uncertainty. 'I'm not trained for anything like that——'

'You are a caring and compassionate person, Melly, and for me that counts far more than any training. You have kept a little bit of your childhood in your heart, and I want that for Jody. I cannot abide the thought of my child growing up to be like her mother, riddled with vanity and engrossed in her appearance. Women such as Irene never realise that beauty is but skin deep, and when such women start to age they become desperate about the little lines around the eyes and the sagging beneath the jaw.'

He faced Melly, his eyes like slits of steel that magnetised her and made her realise how determined he was to make her a party to his plan.

'I must get Jody away from her mother while there is still time—while she is still child enough not to have been unduly influenced by Irene's selfish outlook on life. I desperately need an ally, and I am pleading with you, Melly, to aid me.'

'But you said your wife wouldn't resist if you asked for custody of your daughter,' Melly reminded him.

'I don't think she will to any great degree, but her parents might. They are wealthy New Yorkers and naturally fond of Jody, and I believe they will fight me in the courts when I reveal my intention of taking over the upbringing of my daughter. They will cite me as a divorced man who hasn't remarried in order to provide a regulated home for Jody. They will use their money to have things their way.'

'But what earthly use would I be?' Melly made a helpless gesture with her hands. 'The courts of appeal surely wouldn't regard a child's companion as a good substitute for a mother?'

'Probably not.' He leaned back and sought about in his pockets for his cheroots. He snapped his lighter and not for a second did he take his eyes off Melly's face, almost as if he were dominating her mind and directing her decision.

'It's more than probable,' she tried in vain to evade the steel-like holding of his eyes. 'I'm just an ordinary person who works in the kitchen of a clinic. My education ended when I was sixteen and I haven't had the slightest bit of training in the care of a child. Jody's grandparents would have it all their own way and you know it, Jourdan.'

'Indeed I know it.' Smoke wafted about his face and threaded his dark hair. 'But they wouldn't have all their own way if I took a wife.'

A wife would solve his problem, but Melly wished she didn't have to be the one to hear him say it. 'Then you must do that,' she said, even as something like a claw clutched at her insides. 'How about your friend Caroline's sister, the one who's going to be a bridesmaid?'

His eyes slitted to steel with a smouldering edge. 'That remark was uncalled for and you know it. What I have in mind is that you do me the honour——'

'No——' The claw clutched at her again. 'Ask anyone but me—if you're being serious?'

'Never more serious.' He leaned forward intently. 'You have no commitments of a personal nature, and that job you do can hardly be called a satisfying career. You have to endure the arrogance of women such as Caroline Frome, and the constant sight of people either in their sickbeds or hobbling up and down the corridors in various stages of recovery. I'm filled with wonderment that you remain as cheerful as you do.'

'But I—I couldn't possibly marry you.' Though the very idea made her heart beat with a crazy quickness, her mind thrust a warning sign in front of her. 'No—I don't want to get married—not to you or anyone!'

'Not even if I said that it would be a marriage of convenience? Hear me, Melly! I have been married once and I don't want another experience of that kind, so this second attempt would be a business arrangement so I can present the courts with a *bona fide* wife; a legal companion for my child, a defence that will deflect any arguments put forward by Irene's parents. You will benefit, *ma petite*, in that you will have a house to live in rather than lodgings. You will be able to have fun with Jody, and that is long overdue, eh?'

'But—marriage?' She sat there feeling torn in two, one half of her rejecting what the other half reached for with a lonely eagerness. 'No, I don't think I could——'

'Do you dislike me, Melly?' he asked.

'Of course not——'

'You are acting as if you do.'

So easy, she thought, to let him believe that. A quick nod of the head and he wouldn't mention marriage again, not a man with such a look of pride.

He drew deeply on his cheroot and the smoke had a strong, masculine aroma that made her intensely aware of all that Jourdan represented

... a man who lived dangerously, who had loved other women and who now asked her to share his life.

Big, dark Jourdan Lanier whom she had helped on the road to recovery, and he offered her the chance to see more of the world as his wife ... a chance she couldn't take, could she?

'Jump in at the deep end, Melly,' he urged, as if sensing that she was on the very edge of a decision. 'The Caribbean Sea is blue beyond believing and the water is warm. Do you swim?'

She emphatically shook her head. 'No!'

'Scared of the water as well?'

'Can you wonder that I'm scared of what you're asking of me? We barely know each other——'

'I am sitting here, able to propose to you, because you gave me life.'

'I was glad to be able to do it, Jourdan, but there must be other girls you could ask——?'

'Surely, but they would want what I don't think you do, the intimate side of marriage. True?'

She nodded and looked away from him. 'I suppose you think I'm unnatural?'

'I don't quite know what to think, Melly, but your phobia enables me to ask of you that you marry me in name only.'

'Would it truly be that, or are you only pretending?'

'You have my word of honour, Melly.'

She glanced back at him, studying his forceful face in which his life as a fighting man had engraved its lines. A man who wanted to settle down so he could enjoy the company of his young daughter but who needed a domestic environment so he could lay claim to her.

'I—I am tempted to take the—position,' she said hesitantly.

Jourdan quirked an eyebrow at the word she used, then he inclined his head. 'Yes, that is the best way to regard it, just as a proposition that needs a piece of legal paper. On those terms are we coming to an agreement?'

'It would make a lovely change for me.' A glow was coming into her eyes, warming their colour to the warm sherry he had remarked on. 'It would be nice to be with a youngster—I know I'd like that.'

'You will also like Bel-Aze and the islanders,' he assured her. 'Life in the sunshine makes you feel good inside and out—makes you feel carefree.'

'Bel-Aze,' she murmured. There was a strange, faraway beauty about the name of the island where Jourdan wanted to make his life, where the birds and foliage were of a brilliance never seen in England. Melly felt temptation stirring through her veins, and when Jourdan rose to his feet, raising her so that she stood very close to him for a moment, she had to remind herself that she would be his wife in name only.

She pulled away quickly and went ahead of him out of the smoky saloon bar into the cool night air. She shivered, but it was induced by the excitement burgeoning inside her.

'You are cold.' Jourdan stripped off his jacket and slung its warmth about her shoulders. Melly didn't reject the courteous gesture, hugging the jacket around her and breathing the tang of his cheroots on the cloth.

'There don't seem to be any cabs about.' He glanced up and down the Euston Road. 'We shall have to walk.'

'I don't mind.' Melly glanced up at the sky where the bright stars pierced the infinity of space. 'You can phone for a cab when we reach my flat.'

'I wasn't preparing to stay the night, Melly.'

'No——' she flushed. 'Of course not.'

'You still seem unconvinced that my proposal of marriage is purely based on my need to get custody of my own child.' His footsteps struck the pavement with military precision beside her. 'Probably because you have never been involved in the machinations of people who have more money than they have humanity. While I lay in the clinic I had time to think of Jody in relation to her mother and grandparents who do believe that money can buy anything. But it cannot buy a kind heart, or the sensitivity to be aware of other peoples' feelings, and you have those, *ma petite*, even though you enjoy needling me.'

'I'm sure my needling doesn't penetrate too deeply,' she rejoined.

'Are you implying that I have a thick skin, young woman?'

'You're as tough as leather—except where your little girl is concerned, and that's only natural.'

'Naturally,' he mocked. 'I would not propose to you otherwise.'

'No, you wouldn't,' she reiterated. 'I'm not your type at all. I haven't any glamour and lots of know-how about men.'

'So that's my type, eh?'

'Isn't it?'

'Such women enliven a leave, but I would never tie myself to one of them again. I think I would sooner put my neck in a noose!'

He and Melly walked along side by side, his

step measured to hers. It had been ages since she had been out this late at night, and as they passed the looming archway of a mews she drew a little closer to the tall figure beside her.

'Don't be afraid of marrying me.' Jourdan drew her arm through the crook of his and his fingers enfolded her cold hand. 'I shall keep to the terms of our agreement, I promise you.'

They turned into the road where she lodged, run down over the years and no longer the smart region it had been. 'Bel-Aze will seem like paradise to you.' He spoke with a note of certainty in his voice. 'You will fall in love with the island.'

Paradise, thought Melly, and could well believe it. Not only because of the sun and the palm trees and the bright-winged birds, but because she would see Jourdan every day. They would share the daily joys even if she slept apart from him.

'You can come upstairs for a coffee if you like,' she said, when they stepped into the hall of the house, which was divided into two-roomed flats.

'You are sure?' He had been about to approach the wall telephone in order to call a cab.

'I owe you a coffee,' she said, and was very aware of his tall figure behind her on the stairs. She unlocked the door of her flat and Jourdan followed her into the sitting-room, which she had furnished with items left to her by her grandmother.

'How pleasant!' he exclaimed, for the room had an air of cottage comfort. 'Is that a genuine Windsor rocker that I see?'

Melly smiled as she lit the gas and poured milk into a saucepan. 'Living with my grandmother's furniture makes me feel at home.'

'I can see that it would.' He strolled across to the oak bookcase and stood leafing through a volume or two. 'You seem to have a fondness for horse stories, but I recollect that you worked at a riding-school. Why did you leave what appealed to you to come to London?'

She carefully poured the milk and didn't spill a drop. 'It was around the time I lost my grandmother.'

'Too many memories, eh?'

'Far too many. Do you like your coffee sweet, Jourdan?'

His eyes were upon her face and just a little guarded as they scanned her slim figure in the dress which was simplicity itself and quite unrevealing.

'Had you kept on coming to my room at the clinic, Melly, you would by now have some knowledge of my likes and dislikes. Why did you not come again after that first time? Did I make you shy?'

'Indescribably.' She spoke lightly. 'One spoon or two of sugar, or none at all?'

'One spoon in my coffee, none at all in my tea.'

Melly felt a warming of her skin as she ladled brown sugar into his cup . . . he looked so big and dark, so much the masculine unknown in her small sitting-room. She handed him the cup and he sat down in the rocking chair, long legs stretched across her hooked rug.

'I must arrange to have your belongings shipped out to Bel-Aze,' he said. 'These, after all, are your heirlooms.'

She gave a slight laugh as she sat down on the oak stool upon which Gran had so often rested her weary legs. 'I hadn't thought of it like that.'

'Then you must.' He glanced around the room appreciatively. 'I can see with what good care you take of the things you cherish.'

Cherish, she thought, such a disturbing word on his lips. She looked away from the bold lips of Jourdan Lanier, who said unafraid things and who didn't quite know the depth of her own uncertainty. He saw their marriage in clear-cut terms, and that was because his emotions weren't involved with her. He was concerned only for his daughter and the establishment of a protective and loving relationship in which Jody would feel secure.

He had no real idea of how insecure Melly felt even as she began to accept the idea of marrying him.

'I hope you aren't having second thoughts?'

His voice brushed rich and deep across her disturbed thoughts and Melly felt a brief rush of panic, not unlike the panic she had felt when he had pursued her to the bus stop. She sipped her coffee and after taut moments that stretched into a minute she shook her head.

'I know how much you want to have Jody with you—you have the moral right if your ex-wife wants only to be a social butterfly.'

'That is a good way of putting it.' A frown creased his brow. 'I would not attempt to take Jody into my custody if Irene was a woman with the need to have a child around, but I know for a fact that she leaves Jody with the servants while she goes out having a good time. And she also packs the child off at weekends to stay with her parents, who have this rambling old house on Brooklyn Heights.'

He broke off, muttering a Gallic oath. 'I don't

want my little girl growing up in that way—I want her with me!'

His chin jutted hard and his eyes were brilliant as steel in his Latin face. 'As you say, I have my moral rights, and with your help, Melly, I hope to give Jody a happy, sunlit home where she can be a carefree adolescent instead of a primped version of Irene, or a little old-fashioned copy of her grandmother—if you will forgive the reference? I have an idea your grandmother was a more down-to-earth type to the lady I have in mind, with her lace collars and ropes of pearls and her spine stuffed with dollar bills!'

Melly had to laugh. 'Jourdan——?'

'I am listening, Melly.'

'Why—when did you decide to propose to me?'

'While I was on the island being a convalescent. I was so struck by your unpretentious manner; it was so in contrast to all I remembered of Irene, and I realised that I wanted above all to get Jody away from her mother—as cruel as it might sound. Irene loves herself above all—that I know!'

Jourdan leaned forward, fixing Melly with his steel-grey eyes. 'I knew that in you I had found the right person to assist me. Correct?'

Melly couldn't evade his eyes, nor could she ignore the pounding of her heart. The adrenalin was racing through her veins and she felt more alive than she had felt in a long time . . . a feeling akin to that of galloping a vigorous pony over the Devonshire moors.

'I'll marry you, Jourdan,' she said breathlessly.

Whatever the consequences she wanted to be with him . . . life was lonely without someone to share it with, and even though their marriage was going to be in name only she would do her utmost to make a happy home for Jourdan and his daughter.

Melly felt his sincerity with regard to Jody; she had enough of her grandmother's wisdom in her to recognise that Jourdan was not the sort of man to take Jody away from her mother unless he felt it was to her advantage.

Any doubts which Melly harboured lay within herself . . . within that secret place she couldn't share with the man she had just agreed to marry.

Almost with gravity Jourdan took hold of her hand and pressed his lips into the palm of it. 'Tomorrow I shall buy you a ring for this hand, so have you a favourite gem? Do you like diamonds?'

'Oh, they're far too sophisticated for me——'

'But they are pure, *ma petite*.' His smile was shaded by his own awareness of the world.

'No.' Melly shook her head, feeling sure that he had given diamonds to Irene, who would have expected no less. 'If you feel like kindly giving me a ring, then I rather like the Victorian style. You know, a cluster of tiny pearls forming a sort of flower; something along those lines.'

'Melly, you are a rare girl indeed.' He squeezed her hand. 'We shall be married as soon as everything is arranged, but right now I had better leave you, eh?'

'Yes,' she said, and he was laughing to himself as he left her.

CHAPTER FOUR

MELLY became the wife of Jourdan Lanier in the impressive *salon* at the French Embassy.

A few days previously she had been introduced to Claude Lanier and his wife Marcelle, and despite the importance of their position in London they were a good-natured couple. Claude was several years older than Jourdan and he seemed to accept with diplomatic urbanity his brother's choice of an English girl who was obviously unused to a *milieu* such as he and his wife enjoyed.

The ceremony was quick and simple, and Marcelle had arranged the reception that took place afterwards. The champagne was of the very best vintage, and a delicious buffet was laid out for the guests. Because most of the conversation was in French, Melly stood quietly beside Jourdan and kept sipping champagne in an effort to steady her nerves.

She was actually Madame Lanier and she just couldn't keep her eyes from straying to the dark fascination of Jourdan's profile as he stood laughing and talking with their guests. He looked alarmingly distinguished in his dark blue suit, silk corded shirt and meticulous tie that gleamed like metal. He was so proud and upright, and she came only to his shoulder even though she was wearing shoes with slim high heels.

She still felt dazed by her own daring, and sad that her grandmother wasn't alive to see her married. Yet would Gran have approved of her marrying a man she had known so short a time?

When it was time to leave Melly breathed a sigh of relief. Everyone had been polite, but she sensed that her simplicity had taken these people by surprise ... she instinctively knew that she had been compared to the stylish Irene. In every way she knew herself to be opposite to Jourdan's first wife, the woman who had become so devoted to her own appearance that the marriage had died almost without rancour. Jourdan had assured Melly of this. He and Irene had drifted apart into separate worlds and only Jody had linked them together in the end.

'*Bon voyage!*' Claude leaned into the car to press a small package into Melly's hand. 'Be happy in New York with this brother of mine, and *bonne chance* where the matter of the child is concerned.'

'Many thanks, Claude.' Jourdan shook hands with his brother. 'We shall be in touch. *Au'voir!*'

The big hired car swept into the stream of West End traffic and Melly sat there bemused, holding the small package between her hands. 'Aren't you going to open your present?' asked Jourdan, watching her in some amusement.

'How nice your brother is,' she murmured.

'It runs in the family, I hope.' He spoke drily. 'So now you are Madame Lanier, eh?'

Her heart gave a little lurch inside her, almost of panic, and because she needed to avoid his eyes she began to open the package which Claude had presented to her. The wrapping contained a square leather box, and when she opened the box Melly caught her breath in delight. On a pale satin bed reposed a cross *fleury* of turquoise enamel and silver suspended from a turquoise heart in filigree silver.

'How charming!' Melly exclaimed. 'Just look, Jourdan!'

'That is a *croix à la Jeannette*. It will go well with one of your new dresses, eh? You will dazzle the other passengers on the ship.'

The car was taking them to Southampton, to the dock where the *Queen Elizabeth 2* picked up her passengers. Melly was delighted and quite unable to resist when Jourdan informed her that they were travelling to New York on the famous liner. It was all arranged, their accommodation was booked, and he assured her they would have a wonderful trip on the world's most luxurious cruiser.

His next insistence had been that she go with him to a smart shop in Kensington to select clothes for the voyage, no expense spared because he wanted her to have a chic trousseau. So again she submitted, and quite enjoyed looking at attractive outfits and trying them on. Of course, the assistant didn't approve when Melly firmly told her that she could manage on her own.

'It's customary of our customers to expect assistance.' And beyond the cubicle Melly heard the woman say to Jourdan, 'Madam insists on managing alone, sir.'

'Typical,' he drawled.

Melly could hardly believe that any of these experiences were real, except that the rings on her hand were solid when she touched them, and the man at her side was equally solid in his well-styled suit. Her own outfit was a creamy-beige bouclé suit under which was a silk blouse in a pale-ale colour, and Jourdan had insisted upon giving her a beautiful cashmere coat as a wedding present. Without saying anything he seemed to understand that she abhorred the slaughter of animals in order to glamourise women, so he didn't choose to give her a fur coat. Once again this seemed to signify her total difference from Irene.

For a little while Jourdan sat quiet beside her, as if withdrawn into his thoughts, which she sensed were centred on his daughter rather than on herself. She didn't mind, for it enabled her to study him and get used to the idea that he really was her husband. Even if their marriage was one of convenience it was real enough in the realisation that they had exchanged vows and had a legal document that stated they were man and wife.

Melly sat there quietly in the comfort of the smooth-running car, still holding in her hand the *croix à la Jeannette*, which was a lovely symbol of faith and hope, and belief in the powers of love. Melly could imagine the excitement and glamour which had attended Jourdan's marriage to Irene, who would have worn the traditional satin and lace, and there would have been several brides-maids and ushers and a great many guests, who would have pelted the couple with confetti when they left on their honeymoon.

In a sense this trip on the *QE2* was Melly's honeymoon, but she and Jourdan wouldn't sleep together. The reality of their marriage ended where it usually began for other couples, for whom the actual wedding was only the preliminary to the real delights of their partnership.

For Melly and Jourdan it was the basis on

which he hoped to build a happy relationship
with his daughter.

Through her lashes she watched him and the
breadth of his shoulders under the dark blue
suiting made her very aware of him as a man with
masculine drives and desires. She leaned back in
her seat and sought protection from her own
thoughts by closing her eyes and seeking
relaxation from all the events which had occupied
her since early morning, when she had awoken to
find that her wedding day had arrived ... that
crucial day in any girl's life, fated to bring joy or
regret.

These thoughts produced changing expressions
on Melly's face which she wasn't aware of, then
all at once she felt a touch on her cheek and her
eyes flew open.

Jourdan was leaning over her, studying her
face with a thoughtful look in his eyes. 'Well, my
young bride, we have tied the knot. How does it
feel to have left your old life behind you and to be
embarking on a new one?'

'Still rather strange,' she admitted. 'What
about you, Jourdan? How do you like being a
civilian? Are you sorry to have left the service?'

He considered her question, his eyes straying
over her slender figure in the simple suit and
blouse, a creamy rosebud pinned with a spray of
fern to her lapel. 'I have no regrets,' he assured
her. 'What of you, *ma petite*? *Parfois à tard crie
l'oiseau quand il est pris.*'

'I like it when you speak French,' she smiled,
'but I don't understand a word you're saying.'

'Sometimes,' he translated, 'the bird cries out
too late when in the trap. Do you feel trapped?'

'Not in the least,' she said lightly, but she felt

his shoulders looming above her and knew his body to be trained to the hilt by his years as a military man. He could overpower her physically any time he felt the compulsion, and all she could do was rely on his word of honour, on his promise that their relationship would not be physical.

'Your eyes tell me something else—what wide young eyes you have, and yet a veil of reserve is there; a warning even to me that you will not permit intrusion.' He leaned back as he spoke, withdrawing his closeness as if to let her know that she had no need to fear his desires because she didn't arouse them. In his eyes she was young; a playmate for his daughter, not a mate for himself.

'Are you looking forward to the trip?' he asked.

'Oh yes!' Her eyes lit up. 'I never dreamed I'd ever travel on a ship like the *QE2*. I keep thinking I'm going to wake up and find myself peeling potatoes for dinner at the clinic.'

'You had better pinch yourself, Madame Lanier, for I can assure you I am here beside you and we are well and truly man and wife. At Bel-Aze you will enjoy the delicious dinners that Bethula cooks. She is my cook-housekeeper, a big, warm-hearted islander with a big laugh. At night you will hear the wind whispering in the palm trees—you are going to learn how to swim, that is a priority.'

'I—I used to swim,' Melly tried to keep her voice steady, 'and then I stopped liking it.'

'You will have to start liking the water again.' Abruptly he removed her perky suede hat and threw it aside. 'I like to see your hair uncovered. It has the brightness of a beacon, and it beckoned

me at a time when I was feeling uncertain about
the direction I should take.'

When he spoke like that Melly saw in his eyes
what always looked like a frozen tear, caught and
held in the dark pupils that centred the steely
grey eyes, and it quickened her sympathy that
someone so big and assured should admit to
uncertainty. He had taken her for a wife, and she
had taken him for her husband, but there was a
gulf between them that she didn't dare to bridge.
She held in her sympathy and merely looked at
him with polite interest.

'I expect as a child of the country you were
more at home in the saddle of a moorland pony,
eh?'

'Occasionally Gran and I would take a trip to
the coast in order to enjoy the sea air ... it's
strange how the sea can be so calm one day, and
then all of a sudden be so wild and dangerous.'

'Passion is like that.' His eyes brooded upon
her face as he spoke, his shoulders at rest against
the leather seat, their privacy ensured because of
the glass partition that separated them from the
driver.

Melly tensed ... her every instinct warned her
that Jourdan was a man of strong passions; it was
evident in the thick darkness of his hair, in the
mahogany warmth of his skin, in the depths of
his voice. And with this man she had entered into
a passionless marriage. She wasn't going to be a
real wife to him, and inevitably there would come
a time when she would have to accept that
Jourdan sought the arms of other women for the
solace and excitement of sensuality.

Other women would touch him and kiss him,
and Melly could do nothing about it. She

couldn't expect Jourdan to behave like a monk in bondage to a wife of convenience. It might hurt like hell to envisage him with some other woman, but it was bound to happen.

'Are you glad to have married me?' His eyes were intent, as if he glimpsed in her expression a tinge of sadness. 'You aren't starting to have regrets?'

'You're the one more likely to have regrets, Jourdan, even though you denied them.'

'Because our marriage is not the regulation kind, eh?'

'Yes,' she quietly replied.

'You suspect that I am not *un chevalier sans reproche*?'

'You are a man.' She spoke with a shy kind of dignity. 'I shall understand when you—need a private life.'

'Affairs with women, I expect you mean?'

'Yes. I don't want you to think that I'll ever regard myself as a wife who has the right to—complain.'

'If I should stray?'

'Yes.' Unaware her fingers were gripping the blue and silver *croix* as if she secretly prayed that she would never have to endure his infidelity.

'And what kind of a reaction do you want from me, *petite*, if you do a little straying yourself?'

'But I shan't——!' She looked at him aghast. 'As if I would!'

'But what is sauce for the goose is sauce for the gander, so they say, so if I'm to be on a generous lead where *l'amour* is concerned, why should you not enjoy the same privilege?'

'Jourdan,' Melly gave him an uncertain look, 'are you being serious?'

'Did you imagine for a moment that I was being so?'

'I—I don't know——' Her eyes searched his face. 'Our marriage is unusual a-and I'm not sure about the rules—I just wanted you to know that I don't expect you to give up your way of life just because of me.'

'Because a man has certain needs that you don't wish to share, eh?'

'W-we did discuss that aspect and you said—you promised it would be all right.'

'Now I have you at my mercy, you are worried in case I go back on my word, is that so?' With a brief laugh he caught at her hand and scrutinised the rings which he had put there, the golden band joining the Victorian cluster only a short while ago. 'I rather thought you trusted me, Melly.'

'I do, Jourdan.' The beat of her heart stirred the silk of her blouse. 'I wanted you to know that you aren't tied down because we're married. You're free to do whatever you want, because in a real sense we aren't man and wife, are we?'

'The official who performed the ceremony would be surprised to hear you say so, *petite*.' He spoke drily. 'There are other rooms beside the bedroom in a house that a man and wife share.'

She flushed to the roots of her hair. 'Jourdan, what a naïve fool you must think me!'

'Merely young and rather innocent, but my dear girl, you don't have to keep underlining the fact that I am not to expect any loving from you. Have I yet given a sign that I am panting to have you? Are you expecting to be thrown on the bed as soon as we're alone on the ship?'

Melly's flush stung her skin more deeply. 'I'm very naïve, aren't I?'

'But that is no drawback where Jody is concerned. I want you to be her playmate, is that understood?'

'Yes, Jourdan.' It was both a relief and a pain to hear him say it in such a firm voice.

'Funny child!' He dropped kiss on to her hair. 'You find it hard to believe that something good should happen to you without it all going wrong, isn't that so? You won't believe we are on the ship until you see the ocean all around us, and during those five days on the most beautiful ship in the world we shall get to know each other a little better. We shall become friends. You want that, don't you?'

'Oh yes.' But even as Melly said it, even as she looked at him, her heart seemed to beat painfully against her rib-bones. It was silly to doubt the happiness she felt in being with Jourdan; even if they weren't in love they had married with good intentions. Their reasons weren't specious but had a dusting of gold such as lay over the Hampshire fields as the sun began to burn with the radiance that led to the day's decline.

That smoky-gold sunlight lay over the meadows and woods as if it shone through a great lamp, intensifying the exciting strangeness of her new life.

A short time later the car sped smoothly through the dock area of Southampton and turned in at the gateway, where a policewoman looked at their credentials and directed them to where the great liner lay berthed.

Jourdan shot a glance at his wristwatch. 'There will be certain formalities to go through, but we should be on board by six o'clock and the ship will sail on the evening tide, with a band playing on the dockside to wish us *bon voyage*. We shall enjoy it all from our own private deck.'

Melly gave him an enquiring glance and saw that his eyes were agleam. 'We have the Queen Elizabeth suite,' he told her. 'I was keeping it as a surprise.'

Melly was more than surprised, she was deeply shaken. She had taken it for granted they would have separate cabins, and now he talked of a suite . . . one of the grandest on the ship!

'Aren't you pleased?' he asked casually. 'By the time I booked our accommodation only suites were available—it isn't going to worry you, is it, Melly? The suite is sure to be comfortable.'

'What about the—sleeping arrangements?' she asked quietly.

'There is bound to be a couch.' He gave a brief laugh. 'I'm used to sleeping on a soldier's bed, so I shan't mind. Come on, *petite*, take that affronted look off your face. We are embarking on our honeymoon, remember?'

'It must have occurred to you that I'd mind.' Tears and a touch of fear glittered in her eyes. 'Damn you, Jourdan! I wasn't mistaken in thinking you could be arrogant!'

'Most men can be arrogant, just as most women can be illogical. My dear girl, you are overreacting——'

'I—I trusted you,' she broke in.

'*Mon Dieu*, you really do have a phobia about men, don't you?' He looked exasperated. 'Have you always been so touchy?'

She didn't answer him as the car drew to a stop. She felt and looked rather sick, and Jourdan regarded her with a frown. 'You didn't eat a very substantial lunch, so you are probably hungry,' he said. 'As soon as we go aboard I shall ask the steward for a pot of tea and some sandwiches. You will feel better with some food inside you.'

Still she didn't speak . . . her heart was thudding in her chest and she was seeing images that were torturing her. She walked silently beside him as they went to the reception lounge where boarding cards would be provided. They sat down and she gazed unseeingly in front of her, the excited mill of travellers overshadowed by the mental images that moved through her mind, brought sharply into focus by her realisation that no marriage could be really impersonal.

'Melly, you are behaving as if I've committed a crime!' Jourdan took hold of her hand, an exclamation escaping him when he found it to be extremely cold. Briskly he rubbed some warmth into her fingers. 'I feel insulted, my girl. I'm not going to force myself on you——'

'Let go my hand!' She tried to pull free. 'You've gone and spoiled things, and you were the one who promised they wouldn't be spoiled!'

'You are talking like a child.' His brows meshed across the bridge of his nose, giving him a rather dangerous look. 'I booked this trip in order to please you, do you hear me? It would have been quicker to fly over to New York, but I presumed to think that you might enjoy a short cruise on a luxury liner. I am sorry I bothered if you are going to sulk like this.'

He flung her hand back into her lap, where the rings on it glittered and glowed. A tear fell down the side of Melly's nose and she ached with the misery of not being able to confide in him. Her secret was one she couldn't share with Jourdan . . . no, never with Jourdan!

'Don't cry,' he murmured. 'How could I dream you would be so upset! Later on I shall go and see the Purser and try to change our accommodation. There may have been a cancellation—will that satisfy you?'

'I—I would prefer it,' she said huskily.

'Are you sure you would not prefer to be back in Cinderella's kitchen, peeling the potatoes?' he said, with a touch of sarcasm. 'It surely occurred to you that we would have to share certain parts of our life, even if I made the great sacrifice and kept my urgent hands off your vestal virginity!'

'Don't say such things,' she pleaded. 'You make me feel such a prig.'

'Is that a fact?' The sarcasm deepened in his voice. 'Can you wonder that I think it? I book us into one of the best suites on the ship and you react in this priggish fashion. Any woman in this room would be happy to change places with you.'

'I know I'm being silly,' she mumbled, 'but you just don't understand my feelings.'

'I think I understand them all too well,' he retorted. 'You are a frigid little prude who turns to ice if a man comes anywhere near you. I realise it's the way you are made and I accept that, but what annoys me is that you should think I booked the suite with the ulterior motive of getting into bed with you. To be in bed with a block of ice doesn't arouse my passions, *petite*. A man needs to feel ardent, not frozen, when he makes love to a woman.'

Melly flushed and accepted his scorn. It might annoy him to think she had refrigerated feelings, but it couldn't repel him as the truth could. She crouched away from the very thought, picturing the look on his face if he should ever discover what she kept hidden.

Across the reception lounge a queue was beginning to lengthen at the counter where the boarding cards were being handed out. Jourdan rose to his feet. 'Stay right here,' he said, still with that hard note in his voice. 'I shan't be too long.'

As she watched him walk away Melly was assailed by an urge to dash through the nearest exit; she would soon find a taxi to the railway station and in no time at all she would be on her way back to London. Jourdan would be furious, of course, but it would save them from any more painful clashes of temperament.

Melly half rose from her seat, but it was as if her feet were shackled, for she couldn't move and had to sit down again. Her ringed hand clenched against the left side of her. When Nurse Rosie Wing had learned that Melly was marrying Jourdan she had said, mysteriously, that it had been bound to happen because Melly and Jourdan shared the same bloodstream ... and that was just how it felt, as if in trying to tear herself away from him, she would cause suffering to both of them. He was so looking forward to taking his young daughter to Bel-Aze, where he hoped, with Melly's help, to make a permanent and loving home for her.

It was no use, Melly couldn't endure the thought of letting Jourdan down, not when he was depending on her to support him in his bid to have the upbringing of Jody.

With an effort Melly pulled herself together, so that when Jourdan returned with their boarding cards she had regained some measure of composure.

'People are starting to go on board,' he said. 'Shall we join the scrum—I am eager to see your reaction when you get your first sight of the ship? A few years ago I travelled on her with Irene.'

He said it quite casually, but that didn't stop the name from jabbing Melly like the tip of a dart. Jourdan swung her cashmere coat across his arm and they merged with the crowd that was being slowly absorbed through the doorway that led on to the dockside.

There lay the ship, a great proud beauty from her bow to her stern. Melly stood gazing at the *QE2* with bated breath, and then she and Jourdan began to mount the gangplank that led steeply to the boarding deck. That climb was somehow symbolic for Melly, leading her to the new life she had ventured upon today with a man whose memories of marriage were bound up with another woman.

When he had married Irene he had been a man in love; a man captivated by her glamour and beauty. Even if disillusion had eroded that love and finally worn it away, the memory of it was still there inside him, touched to life again by enjoyments he had shared with her.

And as Melly stepped on board the liner with him, she couldn't help but wonder if he was comparing her looks and her attitude to that of the woman whom Caroline Frome had referred to as stunning.

Melly glanced at Jourdan as they entered the rotunda where they had to wait for their escort to the Queen Elizabeth suite. Was he thinking that on that other trip he had been with a woman eager to share with him all the delights of the voyage? A tall and stunning woman who caught the eye of the ship's officers, clad in her couture clothes and with an air of assurance Melly could never hope to match.

It was strange, but Melly didn't know if Irene had been brunette or blonde, and though Jourdan no longer cared for her, she had borne his child, and always when he mentioned Jody there was a look of tenderness in his eyes.

Right now he glanced about him as if in the grip of memories that excluded Melly, and when he finally looked at her, his eyes were a cool grey. No warmth came into them as he ran his gaze over her hair . . . he didn't seem to see it as bright like gold any more.

Gold was warm and Jourdan looked at her as if she made him feel cold.

'Nothing has changed,' he said. 'The ship is still as I remember her, with an atmosphere entirely her own. Does it excite you to be one of her passengers?'

'Very much,' Melly replied, and wished she could cast aside inhibition and link her arm through his. She longed to tell him how much he meant to her, but instead she had to let him believe that being married to him in name only was all she desired.

CHAPTER FIVE

MELLY wandered around the Queen Elizabeth suite, amazed by the glamour of its décor and furniture. The bed was king-size with a luxurious coverlet that reached to the thick creamy-coloured carpet. There was a large closet for clothing and a vanity table with a big round mirror lit by lamps.

A curve of steps led to a lounge which opened on to the private deck which Jourdan had mentioned. When Melly mounted the little staircase she found the lounging area furnished with a cocktail cabinet, a record player and an L-shaped couch piled with cushions.

She sighed incredulously, and pushed open the strong door that led to the deck where a pair of canvas loungers waited to be used, a table placed between them. There were also several matching canvas chairs, presumably for guests.

The deckside was rather high, so Melly climbed on to a wooden bench in order to see what was going on down on the dock. Piles of baggage were being swung into the hold of the ship and already lights were dancing on the water and members of the crew were coming aboard. There were small groups of onlookers down on the stone paving of the dock, awaiting the arrival of the bandsmen who would play a rousing selection of music as the ship made her stately way out to sea, her great tonnage towed manfully by the much smaller tugs, their tootings and hootings mingling with the music of the brass band.

One of the persons down below waved to Melly and she waved back, a lump coming into her throat. There was no telling when she would see England again, for Jourdan hoped to take Jody with them straight to the Caribbean.

Right now he was with the Purser trying to arrange what he had promised Melly, a change of accommodation so that she could have the privacy that meant so much to her. Her fingers clenched the deck rail and she breathed the sea coolness in the air, watching the shore lights brighten as the sky darkened. Suddenly she gave a shiver that was a mixture of excitement and chill.

'Put this on.' In his lithe and silent way Jourdan had joined her on the deck and he slid her cashmere coat around her shoulders. 'You will feel cold as the ship gets under way.'

'Will it be soon?' She snuggled into the coat that was so smooth and warm.

He leaned on the deck rail and his profile was dark and strong against the dusk light. 'The band will strike up and the tugs will start us on our way. Splendid ship, is she not?'

'She's a dream ship,' Melly breathed, wondering why he didn't tell her the outcome of his visit to the Purser. Was he tormenting her a little because he thought her insistence on privacy both priggish and insulting?

His lighter clicked and the smoke of his cheroot drifted into the night air. '*Je regrette*,' he said quietly, 'but you must endure my company for the next few nights. I could have shared a cabin on a lower deck, but I am not that gallant, my lady. If you are afraid of arousing my passions if I should catch sight of you in your lingerie, then let me remind you that I didn't marry you for your body—which you guard as if it were a rare piece of sculpture bound for the Louvre!'

His sarcasm stung even as Melly admitted to herself that it would have been beyond the call of duty for him to deny himself the comfort of the lovely suite he had paid for. She had hoped, in fact, that he might arrange other accommodation for herself, but she bit back her insistence that he do this. His cool, ironic tone of voice assured her that he wouldn't touch her . . . hadn't she seen the pride in him that day at the clinic when she met him for the first time?

As the military band played *We Are Sailing*, sparkling lights streamed down into the water, the soft magic of twilight veiling the daylight shabbiness of the docks. The liner made her queenly way out to sea and as the music gradually faded into the distance, and the tugs cast themselves loose, the wind whipped up and blew Melly's hair against Jourdan's shoulder.

She stood there mutely as the last strains of the music were lost in the darkness. 'Quite a moment,' Jourdan murmured.

'Yes.' Melly wondered if he was thinking of that other occasion when he had stood with a woman and listened to fading echoes of music across the water. Had they embraced and made promises they had passionately meant to keep?

'Our journey begins.' His eyes swept Melly's pensive face, a pale outline just below his shoulder, her hair ruffled by the wind. 'Let us go inside and have a cup of tea. I feel sure you are longing for that more than for anything else.'

'I hope I'll be a good sailor.' She felt the movement of the ship as they crossed the deck. Inside the suite the lamplit cosiness made her feel more secure. She slid her coat from her shoulders and was about to pour out the tea when Jourdan ordered her to sit down and relax. She watched him pour the tea and thought how serious his face looked in the lamplight. She felt a tug of nerves inside her and sensed what was going through his mind . . . that she was a prudish companion for a man to have with him on a cruise.

He sat down on the couch after handing her a cup of tea, but left quite a bit of space between them. The tea was hot and sweet and Melly relished it.

'Dinner is at eight-thirty.' Jourdan munched a sandwich. 'We don't dress formally the first night at sea, so we can afford to relax for a while. You don't mind too terribly that we have to share this suite, do you?'

Melly shook her head. She had accepted the situation and didn't want to do further damage to his estimation of her. 'It's very glamorous and must have cost you an awful lot of money.'

'Quite so.' His lips quirked. 'I'm not exactly a rich man, but I inherited shares in the canning company owned by my father's family. The interest from the shares was well invested, and that is how I can afford a house at Bel-Aze with a banana plantation attached. I'm hoping to make the plantation a paying concern, though it's very run down at present and needs a lot of work. How do you fancy being a planter's wife?'

'I—I hope you don't feel cheated, Jourdan?' The words broke from her. 'I know you think I'm—odd.'

'Had I wanted a regular type of marriage, Melly, I would have sought one. You have become distressed over this matter of the suite, as if it were a deliberate ploy of mine to force you into an intimate relationship. I don't use those kind of tactics with any woman, do you understand me?'

'Yes,' she said quietly.

'Then do relax.' He gave the couch an appreciative pat. 'I shall sleep very well on this, having slept on the ground quite a number of times, I do assure you. The Army doesn't encourage gracious living.' He glanced around the lounging area with appreciation. 'Very grand indeed. I wonder how many stars of stage, screen and the music world have made use of this suite?'

'Didn't you have one of these suites when you travelled with Irene on the *QE2*?' Melly found herself asking him.

'She would have liked it,' he said quizzically, 'but at that time they were fully booked, so we had to travel in a less glamorous cabin.'

'Is she very attractive?' Melly couldn't suppress the compulsion that made her want to know.

'Let us say she works at it,' he said, with irony. 'You will look equally attractive in your new dresses, so stop worrying and enjoy yourself— you are such an anxious young thing, aren't you, Melly?'

'Yes,' she agreed, with a deprecating laugh. 'I'm sorry if I annoy you with my—phobia.'

'You know what the cure entails, don't you?' He lounged among the couch cushions and there was a gleam of devilry in his eyes. '*Mon Dieu*, but there is no need to sit there so rigidly beside me.

Have I not promised that I shall treat you as if
you are my child?'

'Some men wouldn't be quite so generous,' she
said, and was amazed by her ability to look
composed when everything about him disturbed
her so much. Any normal bride would be in his
arms right now, but she sat withdrawn from him
into the corner of the couch.

'Meaning they would want their pleasure?'

She nodded and the colour of her eyes
deepened as if taking his darkness into them.

'We are going to make the most of every
moment of this trip,' Jourdan said decisively.
'When we reach New York the battle begins . . . I
have wired Irene to let her know my plans. I've
informed her of my marriage to you, Melly, and
made it plain that I want the upbringing of
Jody. I feel fairly confident about the outcome,
but what are your feelings, eh?'

'I'm praying it will all work out as you've
planned, Jourdan. I know how disappointed
you'll be if—if something goes wrong.'

Jourdan stared into her eyes, a conflict of
emotions chasing each other across his features.
'What are you thinking—tell me!'

'Irene may not like it that you've remarried.'

'The devil she won't!' His chin hardened.
'There is nothing left of what we had together, so
why should she mind?'

Melly hesitated. 'Vanity may do it. You
belonged to her, and now you belong to—to
someone else. Vain people are egocentric, aren't
they? They can't imagine that they can be
replaced.'

He sat there frowning in thought, and Melly
decided that it might be wise if she left him alone

to consider a tougher fight for Jody than he
anticipated. She quietly left him sitting there and
went down the little staircase to the bedroom,
where she collected her robe and toiletries and
went into the bathroom, where she quietly slid
the bolt.

Her tenseness gradually soaked away in the
lemon-scented water that covered her to the
shoulders. She lay back relaxed and told herself
there was a chance of happiness with Jourdan so
long as Jody was placed in his custody without
too much of a struggle. Together with the child
they would be a family.

Water splashed as she climbed out of the bath
and reached for her towelling robe. Thoughts of
the past and the present moved in and out of her
mind as she stood brushing her teeth, the motion
of the ship beneath her feet. She had just rinsed
her mouth and replaced the cap on her toothpaste
when a strong heave sent her lurching across the
bathroom, and before she could grasp something
solid she fell and hit her arm against the side of
the bath.

'Dammit!' She sat there on the floor nursing
her arm, her nerves jolting as knuckles rapped
upon the door.

'Are you all right in there?' Jourdan loudly
demanded.

'Yes—I dropped something——'

'From the sound of it yourself—open this door
to me!'

'I'm perfectly all right.' She scrambled to her
feet. 'Give me a few more minutes, then you can
have the bathroom.'

When she slid back the bolt and stepped
outside she was startled to find Jourdan waiting

for her. 'What happened?' he asked. 'I heard you cry out—did you slip getting out of the bath?'

'The ship gave a heave and I knocked my arm.' She went to pass him, but he blocked the way and she drew back against the wall, intimidated by how big he was when he came close to her.

'Show me your arm,' he ordered.

'It isn't anything——'

'Let me look.'

Reluctantly she drew back her sleeve and he took her arm in his fingers and scrutinised the bruise which had formed. 'The bone feels intact, but that bruise looks painful.'

'My bruises always look dramatic.' Melly smiled nervously and edged her robe more closely around her.

Jourdan stared down at her, then quite unexpectedly he raised her arm and brushed the bruise with his lips. 'Kiss and make it better,' he murmured. 'Mmmm, you smell of lemons.'

'I—I've left my bath-gel in the bathroom and you're welcome to use it,' she said, feeling the thud of her heart as he continued to look down into her eyes.

'Nervous as a cat, aren't you?' he said mockingly.

'I—I've never been on a ship before.'

'What you really mean is that you have never been alone like this with a man before.' And looking sardonic, he let her go and strolled into the bathroom.

Melly made sure she was fully dressed by the time Jourdan rejoined her, looking refreshed from what had obviously been a vigorous shower. Scrolls of damp hair clung to his forehead and he had a subtle foreign air about him, reminding her of all the differences between them. She felt his eyes looking her up and down as he buttoned himself into a clean white shirt.

She was wearing a frilled satin shirt in ivory with narrow black trousers, and her hair had a dazzling brightness in contrast to her creamy skin and honey-coloured eyes. She had made an effort to look her best, but she didn't imagine for one moment that she looked as stunning as Irene would have looked.

While Jourdan fitted oval gold links into his cuffs, Melly sat on the foot of the bed and buffed her fingernails. Her work at the clinic had caused her to have dishpan hands and they didn't go very well with her lovely rings.

She held out a hand and studied the result of her buffing. 'You will find a beauty salon on the ship,' Jourdan told her. 'I would suggest that you take those rather unlovely hands to the salon for some professional attention.'

'Are they very awful?' Melly bit her lip. 'Washing pots and pans isn't very kind to the hands.'

'Melly,' he stood looking down at her in his stylish suit, that slightly ironic look on his face, 'for your own sake, child, don't go telling all about yourself to some of the women you will meet on the ship. You are my wife and that is sufficient, do you understand me?'

'I was poor but honest.' Her smile wavered. 'I'm afraid I can't do much about my unworldly ways, and you said you didn't mind.'

'I don't, but snobs abound on cruises—for some curious reason—and such people can be patronising and hurtful.'

'So what do I say if anyone asks what I did for my living before I married you?' She gazed up at him, looking ingenuous despite her Pucci shirt and perfume to match.

'Merely say that you worked in a hospital.'

'So they'll assume I was a nurse?'

'Is that so bad?'

'Are you ashamed of being married to the kitchen help?' Melly asked.

'No,' he frowned, 'I wish to protect your feelings.'

'Don't you really mean your own feelings, Jourdan?'

His eyes glittered, a warning that she was putting an edge on his temper. 'You look very chic, *ma petite*, and I won't have the wives of butchers and greengrocers patronising my wife. Given half a chance and they will do it, you can take my word for it. I've been around and I know the ways of women.'

'I expect you do.' Melly wasn't ashamed of her work at the clinic and she felt like reminding Jourdan that if she hadn't been working in the kitchen when he was admitted for his emergency operation, then he might not have survived.

'I know what you are thinking, Melly.' He jammed his fists into the pockets of his jacket. 'It's because I owe my life to you that I don't want you to be a target for those who like to be spiteful. You are a non-aggressive person, which doesn't mean that you aren't spirited and self-reliant. It means that you don't care to hurt the feelings of other people, but there are those who get their pleasure from it. You have met them!'

'Women like Caroline Frome, I suppose you mean?' Melly tilted her chin. 'I'm not such a mouse, Jourdan, that I run squeaking when I'm confronted by a cat.'

'I recall,' he said drily, 'that you ran from the Ritz.'

She flushed slightly. 'I—I wasn't running away from Caroline Frome.'

'I see,' his eyes filled with Gallic amusement, 'you were running away from me. Are you pleased that I caught up with you?'

She nodded, for how could she deny to herself that every vital inch of him had become of inestimable value to her ... it was her secret, of course, and she was good at keeping secrets.

'Be on your guard,' he said seriously, 'for even in a Pucci shirt and perfume you look young enough to be my daughter.'

'You must have started young!' she retorted.

'Who is arguing with you?'

'I can take care of myself without telling lies, Jourdan.' She met his amused gaze. 'I'll give as good as I get—snooty women don't scare me.'

'Perhaps not.' Jourdan raised her to her feet and gave her a very intent look. 'There never was a girl quite like you, Melly. I can never decide if you are utterly forthright or extremely devious. To look at you have a fine simplicity, but I suspect it to be a shield and a very impenetrable one. I wonder what your secret is?'

'My—secret?' She managed a slight laugh. 'What makes you think I have one?'

'It's there,' he touched her face, 'just beyond those wide eyes.'

'It's just me looking hungry,' she said lightly.

'Let us go to dinner, then.' He locked the door of the suite and they walked along the carpeted passage that led past the steward's pantry to the stairs leading down to the Queen's Grill Bar.

'Fancy a cocktail before we go to the restaurant?' asked Jourdan.

'Please.' Melly felt the acceleration of her pulse as they walked into the bar and female eyes focused upon Jourdan, then upon herself. Those eyes appraised her outfit and hairstyle in the frankly hostile way of women who want to find fault with anyone younger than themselves, especially if she happens to be accompanied by an attractive man. Without even glancing around the bar at the men in it, Melly knew that Jourdan had a force and a style that put them in the shade. The thought made her glow and hold her head high.

He found a pair of seats and beckoned the bar steward. 'Two champagne cocktails,' he requested, and Melly sensed an added stirring of interest among the women when he revealed his French accent.

She smiled to herself, but her fingers squeezed her evening purse when she saw one of the women giving her a probing look, as if trying to work out her relationship to Jourdan. As casually as possible Melly draped her left hand on the table top and displayed the rings on the third finger.

The woman probed about in a dish of nuts and her own hands were plump, their tips scarlet with lacquer, heavy-stoned rings embedded in the flesh. Her gaze slid to Jourdan and she actually fluttered her eyelashes at him. Melly watched as one of the fat little hands slid the bowl of nuts towards him.

'Do take one,' she said. 'They do keep us waiting for dinner, don't they? I'm absolutely famished—whoops!'

The ship gave another of those startling undulations that reminded her passengers that they were heading into the Atlantic.

'All right, *chérie*?' Jourdan curled an arm around Melly, making it plain to everyone that she was his property. The gesture thrilled her in public as much as it would have alarmed her had she been alone with Jourdan. She knew his motive; he was a proud man who didn't intend his wife to be overawed by the more experienced travellers on the ship. He made her feel protected and rather special, and though she sat demurely within the circle of his arm, the very touch of him was a deep and very secret delight.

When the steward brought their cocktails Jourdan clinked his bowl against Melly's and looked into her eyes. 'May all that we hope for be realised,' he murmured. 'But for the next few days we think only of having fun.'

'To fun,' she smiled.

They were seated at a fairly large table for dinner and first-name introductions were made. It was rather like a party, Melly thought, and as she gazed around her it seemed incredible that they were on the high seas. People were ordering their wine and selecting their food with such aplomb, as if every day of their lives they sat at a ship's table and felt the motion of the ocean beneath their feet.

'The food on the menu looks scrumptious,' said the girl directly facing Melly. She was bright and friendly and had said her name was Brenda, but the friend she was travelling with had a rather sullen expression, unenlivened by the high-necked sweater she was wearing.

'I fancy just about everything,' Brenda enthused.

'For God's sake don't choose everything,' her friend snapped, 'or you'll be up all night paying visits to the bathroom.'

'It could well be worth it,' mused Brenda, shooting a smile at Melly. 'What is *flambé bon filet?*'

Jourdan enlightened her and she widened her eyes at him. 'You're French!'

'I have that honour,' he smiled.

'Both of you?' Brenda's eyes dwelt on Melly's very fair hair.

'My wife is English.'

'How romantic!'

'You are an advocate of romance?' he asked.

'What woman isn't?' Brenda gave a little laugh, and then as if his grey eyes confused her, she glanced at Melly. 'I can't help admiring your rings; the gold band looks brand new, so I take it your marriage is in the same condition?'

'We haven't been married for very long,' Melly admitted, hoping that Jourdan wouldn't tell their fellow diners that they were newlyweds. The thought of a couple on their honeymoon seemed to trigger off all sorts of innuendoes, and as things stood between Jourdan and herself it would be rather embarrassing to have everyone looking at them and picturing their passionate embraces.

Fortunately Jourdan took his cue from the swift, rather imploring glance she gave him. He smoothly turned the subject back to food, and in a short while Melly was enjoying a delicious slice of fish served in a creamed mushroom sauce. Their wine was a Puligny-Montrachet, pale gold with a subtle flavour of hazelnuts, and before long the atmosphere at the table was very convivial.

One of their companions was a man named Clifford who travelled quite a lot and admitted to being a fairly successful writer of crime stories. He said with a lazy smile that money was at the root of most crimes but in his opinion the passions between men and women led to the more interesting ones.

'I hope you don't intend to use any of us in one of your books?' The question came from the rather stiff-necked woman who sat beside a genial-looking man with a Czar Nicholas moustache and beard.

'Would you be very annoyed?' Clifford wanted to know, shrewd eyes glinting behind horn-rimmed glasses.

'Indeed I would, young man.' The woman's neck seemed to grow even stiffer. 'My husband and I aren't the kind of people to get involved in anything criminal.'

'Misfortune, dear lady, can happen to any of us, given the correct circumstances. We all have passions, and they're more in control of us than we are in control of them.'

'Not at our age,' the woman asserted. 'Arthur and myself are well past the stage of having passions, thank you very much.'

Arthur spooned his consomme and looked as if he was quite used to having his passions put away in mothballs by his truculent wife, while Brenda said excitedly:

'I wouldn't mind being in your book, Clifford. I think it would be fun.'

'So long as you were not the victim?' Jourdan enquired.

'Oh no, I wouldn't want to be a victim,' she laughed, 'but I wouldn't mind being the detective's girl-friend.'

'My detective,' Clifford smiled, 'is a large man of sixty who drinks Guinness, drives a veteran Bentley and is an authority on Roman ruins. His own passions, he asserts, have long been in ruins.'

'He sounds a pet to me,' said Brenda. 'I happen to like older men.'

'You make me laugh, Bren.' Her friend. 'You're supposed to be a supporter of the feminist movement, yet every time you open your mouth it's obvious that you're dying to be shackled to some man!'

'Is that so dreadful?' asked Jourdan. 'Don't you think we men are very nice to be shackled to?'

'Naughty is a better word for it!'

'Do you so disapprove of naughtiness?' he wanted to know. 'This feminist movement intrigues me, for what do you hope to achieve from it? Total self-sufficiency?'

'At any cost,' was the defiant reply.

'It could cost you—love,' he rejoined.

'Men aren't interested in *love*.' The note of defiance had risen in the girl's voice. 'Modern women have found that out with a vengeance, and we aren't so ready any more to be playthings while men go merrily on their way enjoying the apple while Eve eats the core!'

'Tough talk,' Jourdan mocked. 'Do you truly believe what you are saying, or are you quoting from a book written by someone who is probably having a good time herself while exploiting the emotional problems of other women ... stirring them up because they have curves instead of muscles.'

'That's all you men ever think about, curvy girls exposed on posters and calendars!'

'And very nice, in my opinion.' Jourdan sampled his roast duck and creamed truffle. 'So the feminists are determined to change the order of things. You hope to assume the dominant role, eh? Do you think you can?'

'We'll have a good try.'

'If that is your fancy, *mon enfant*, then by all means enjoy it.'

'It's no fantasy, and trust a man to laugh!'

'I don't think many of us will be laughing if your movement ever succeeds.' Jourdan glanced at Melly, who was contentedly eating her own dinner and about as interested in the feminist movement as she was in riding to hounds in order to see a fox mauled to pieces. 'What do you make of all this, *chérie*? Do you support the damnation of the male sex?'

'If I did, Jourdan, then I wouldn't have married you.' She forked tender calves' liver into her mouth and looked him in the eye. 'I don't mind if you're a chauvinist.'

'Most women want a husband before they want anything else,' declared the woman who had managed to make hers very humble despite his luxuriant moustache and beard. 'It's those who can't get one who talk all this feminist claptrap!'

'I don't know about that,' said Melly, 'but how many women would really want to crawl along dark tunnels to dig out coal? And how many could handle one of those horrible road drills? I can think of lots of jobs that would knock women out.'

'I have an idea, Melly, that the feminists are planning to be the governors,' Jourdan said sardonically. 'They are going to sit behind the desks and direct the digging and drilling—is that not so, you two young women?'

'Don't mix me up with Olive,' Brenda pleaded. 'She goes a little too far in her ideas——'

'You infuriate me, Bren.' Olive looked it. 'Silly romantic ideas have helped men to gain control over women, who only ever love themselves. But one day it will be a new sort of world and men will learn what it feels like to be the underdogs!'

'And will the women fight the wars?' asked Jourdan, and Melly heard the steely hardening of his voice. 'Or in this new order of things are the men still to be expected to have their heads blown off, but this time for the privilege of being the underdogs of women *sans* mercy, *sans* charm, *sans* everything that makes their company a pleasure instead of a pain in the neck?'

There was an acute silence around the table, then Brenda spoke with a catch in her voice: 'Please don't let us fall out over Olive's stupid ideas. When she gets a bee in her bonnet there's no shifting it—oh, look, here comes the dessert trolley! Oh, isn't it a picture!'

The tension relaxed and Melly breathed a sigh of relief. Knowing that Jourdan had been a serviceman she realised that he had seen some of his comrades die in the course of duty, and that stupid girl in the mannish sweater wasn't worth his anger. She was callow and unimaginative and needed a giddy romance of her own to bring her to her senses.

'What are you thinking about in such a serious way, *ma petite*?' Jourdan's voice broke in softly on her thoughts.

'Whether to have strawberries and cream, or *crêpes Suzette*.' She felt her lips shake a little when she smiled at him. 'Which do you suggest?'

'Both are delicious.' His gaze dwelt a moment on her mouth. 'Why not have *crêpes Suzette* tonight and the strawberries tomorrow night? We shall be on the ship for several days.' There was a note of indulgence in his voice, as if at times she seemed to him little older than his daughter Jody.

Brenda decided on *crêpes Suzette* as well, and they watched with fascination as their dessert was prepared, devil-blue flames shooting into the air as the folded pancakes were turned in the sauce and served *flambé* on their plates. Melly tasted hers, aware that Jourdan was watching her, the dark lashes across the grey irises, his expression lazily intent.

'Mmm, it's heavenly, with a tang of tangerines.' Her own eyes were slumbrous at the taste. 'I never realised that food could taste so good—by the time we reach New York I shall look like Bessie Bunter!'

Jourdan merely smiled and ate his Camembert and crackers.

'Would you mind, Jourdan, if I started to look like a pudding?' she couldn't resist asking.

'Who expects to look like a pudding?' Brenda wanted to know.

'My wife,' Jourdan replied.

'Don't tell me you two are expecting a happy event?' Brenda gazed avidly at Melly. 'Are you pleased?'

'But I'm not——' Melly had flushed deeply.

'Go on with you!' Brenda wagged her fork. 'That blush is enough to give away your little secret.'

'Jourdan,' Melly appealed, 'say something!'

'I wonder,' he said, glancing around the table, 'who is going to win the sweepstake?'

While the men discussed the lottery Melly had to sit there being studied with that half-envious curiosity which attacked some women the moment they believed themselves in contact with a woman whom a man had impregnated.

There was something almost primitive about it, and in Melly's view it made mincemeat of the feminist idea that women could do anything the male of the species could do.

She stole a look at Jourdan and indulged in the fantasy of wondering what it would be like to be having his child. Strong, self-reliant men were often the best sort of fathers, and there was no doubt about his affection for Jody. Melly was looking forward to meeting her, but she had no intention of trying to behave like a mother to Jody. That was Irene's status in the child's life and it mustn't be interfered with. What Melly hoped for was to establish a companionship that Jody could rely upon and enjoy.

Jourdan had said there was an excellent school on the island and his daughter would attend as a day pupil. He was set on making a happy home for her, and Melly was determined to help him succeed. She could never put out of her mind the fact that he had resigned from the Army and married someone he wasn't in love with in order to take care of Jody.

It might amuse him to play the fond husband in front of their fellow diners, but everyone had a public mask and a private one, and she had tried his temper when she had reacted against sharing a suite with him. His annoyance had been justified ... how could he be expected to understand her reluctance when he didn't know what lay at the root of it?

Her secret must stay locked up in her heart even though she had to face up to the fact that she was in love with Jourdan. She could no longer deny his effect on her emotions; the message sped to her heart whenever he looked at her with those grey eyes beneath the thick dark hair with a kind of stallion's coat gloss to it.

She couldn't let herself imagine what it might be like to be crushed to him in passion, his mouth dominating hers, drivingly warm and desirous as it moved over her skin.

Melly thrust away the thought of being kissed and caressed . . . least of all must she be touched by Jourdan.

A resolve easy enough to think about but difficult to put into practice when he decided to take her dancing in the ship's ballroom when he discovered that Lew Martin's orchestra was providing the dance music.

'We shall dance in the old-fashioned way to that kind of music,' he explained, which meant that she spent the next few hours locked in his arms, gliding around the floor to such nostalgic tunes as *The Very Thought of You*, and *My Foolish Heart*.

It was after midnight when they made their way to the Queen Elizabeth suite . . . a lithe man with lazy eyes holding the hand of a fair-haired girl who felt enjoyably tired, her mind filled with sentimental words which the vocalist had sung while the lights dimmed and the couples dreamily danced.

If only her foolish heart would be still instead of beating so fast as she and Jourdan mounted the stairs that led to where their suite was situated, at the very end of a passage that couldn't go on for ever, to a door that had to be reached and unlocked, into the intimacy they must share.

The lamplight inside illumined the enormous bed, with the covers neatly turned back, Melly's nightwear laid alongside dark silk pyjamas. She stood there indecisively, fiddling with her rings and praying for Jourdan to make the situation easy for her.

'Stop shivering.' His hands clasped her shoulders, a touch of temper in them. 'I shall go and play cards for a while and give you time to settle down.'

'I—I'm sorry, Jourdan,' her body was alive with tension. 'I can't help the way I am——'

'I realise that.' He drew his hands away from her. 'Go to bed, and don't worry so. Would you like me to order you a cup of Horlicks—it might settle your nerves.'

'No, thank you.' She detected the ironic note in his voice. 'Dancing has tired me—I'll soon sleep.'

'We had a good time, eh? You dance well for a girl who hates men to touch you.'

She flushed and avoided his eyes. 'You're easy to follow, Jourdan. I enjoyed myself.'

'Then won't you give me the smallest good-night kiss?'

Startled, she looked at him, and swiftly he bent his head and kissed her on the mouth. 'There, did that give you a heart attack?'

He couldn't know as he left her standing there that her heart was in a turmoil, and she didn't relax until the door closed, sinking slowly down on the bed in order to relieve her trembling legs.

She didn't know what her reaction would have been had he insisted on staying. Had he suddenly

revoked his earlier promises and wanted his
rights as a husband.

All during the dancing the thought had been in
her mind. Jourdan had held her possessively close
to him and she had been almost unbearable aware
of the pressure of his body through the fabric of
her clothes. Dancing with him had been a very
sensuous experience and she was still conscious
of the feelings it had evoked as she sat there alone
in the softly glimmering lamplight.

Oh God . . . she pressed her face into her
hands. Things had to work out right where Jody
was concerned, for though she loved Jourdan
right through to her bones she couldn't be a real
wife to him.

The very thought of being so drove her to her
feet, her eyes wild with pain and torment.

She loved him . . . loved everything about him,
from head to heel, but the physical act of love was
something she was unable to face. There was no
way she could give herself bodily to Jourdan . . .
all she could give him was her heart, beating as if
through bars as she pressed her hand to her left
side.

She could only cherish him here in her heart.

CHAPTER SIX

JOURDAN didn't say much on the flight to the Caribbean, and his silence spoke volumes so far as Melly was concerned.

After disembarking from the ship they had gone straight to their hotel in Manhattan, where a message awaited him from his American lawyer. It contained the information that Irene had remarried, and as Jourdan stood there holding the message, Melly had seen his chin turn as hard as rock, and when he finally looked at her the light of expectation had gone out of his eyes.

He told her that Irene had taken for her second husband one of the wealthiest brokers on Wall Street, a man who was willing to accept her daughter as his own.

Slowly Jourdan had crushed the sheet of paper into a ball and tossed it away from him, and Melly realised that he had accepted the fact that he could no longer fight Irene for the custody of Jody. Within a few days they left New York and were now on their way to Bel-Aze, just the two of them, his daughter left behind in America with her mother and stepfather.

On their way to the airport Jourdan had said to Melly: 'She's done it on purpose. She knew how much I wanted Jody with us, so she has stopped me in my tracks.'

'Can't you fight her?' asked Melly. 'After all you are Jody's natural father.'

He shook his head. 'No, I am not going to turn

Jody into a tug-of-love child, that would not be fair on her.'

His reply was no more than Melly expected of him; she knew his strength of will and his integrity, and the worry uppermost in her mind was what this turn of events would do to their marriage. There no longer seemed a reason for it. Jourdan hadn't married her for love; she had been his weapon as he prepared to fight for the custody of Jody; a fight he now abandoned because he didn't want his love for the child to be damaged.

Melly sat quietly beside him on the aircraft, gazing from the window at the enormous banks of snowy cloud, wondering what their life would be like at the plantation house ... two people locked into a marriage whose foundation had no substance to support it. There seemed only one thing she could do and that was to suggest that they apply for an annulment, making it possible for them to say goodbye without regrets ... on his side, at least.

Even as the words trembled on her lips Jourdan placed a hand over hers, pressing her fingers until she felt his rings digging into her bones. 'Stop looking so worried,' he said. 'Admittedly our plans were centred on Jody living with us, but we can try and make a life together. The way things have turned out is disappointing for both of us, but I feel sure you will like Bel-Aze, and you will enjoy giving the plantation house your personal touch. Come, I don't like to see you looking so pensive.'

'I—I don't want to impose myself on you.' Her eyes dwelt large and grave on his face. 'Our marriage can be annulled without any problems——'

He shook his head. 'No, I don't wish you to go back to that life you were living before we met. There is no need of that. What I want is to try and make the plantation a paying concern—think what a challenge it will be!'

When she saw a little of the light returning to his grey eyes Melly relaxed and decided to let him make the decisions where their marriage was concerned. She didn't want to be lonely and her heart shrank from the possibility of never seeing him again, and inevitably that would happen if she made it seem that she wanted him to apply for an annulment.

'Is it a large house?' she asked.

'I consider it to be so. It has an enormous verandah that envelops it on all sides so that in the morning you can take breakfast in the sunlight and in the evening watch the sun go down, with a long cool drink.' He ran his gaze over Melly. 'You will have to protect that skin of yours, otherwise some of those flying insects will make a meal of you. You are not too much afraid of beetles and spiders, are you?'

'Spiders?' she exclaimed, her skin crawling at the thought of tropical ones. 'I'm afraid I can't stand them!'

'Then if you see one you will have to let out a yell and Bethula will come to your rescue. You are bound to like her; she's a good soul, not over-keen on housework but a first rate cook. She has converted me to island dishes; some of them are rather spicy, but I have a soldier's stomach. I don't know if you enjoy spicy foods, Melly, but you ate very well on the ship, though I am glad to see that you aren't looking like Bessie Bunter.'

She smiled, and then looked confused at the

way Jourdan intently watched her, studying the
ebb and flow of colour that her fair skin couldn't
conceal.

'Are you very upset over Jody?' she asked
quickly, fending off the perplexity she aroused in
him.

'You worry about other people's feelings, don't
you, Melly? I find such concern much of a
novelty after Irene, who never worried about
anyone except herself. Yes, I should have liked
Jody to grow up on the island; it would have been
a carefree, healthy life, eating good fresh food and
mixing with all sorts of children. As it is she will
grow up in the environment which suits Irene,
and I must let it happen. It does children no good
to be fought over, for the term tug-of-love is an
exact one and the child involved feels she is being
pulled in two directions at once. *Non*, I won't
have that for Jody! Let her remain where she is,
and I can but hope that she has enough strength
of character to become her own person.'

He sat silent for some moments, still gripping
Melly's hand, then he said quietly: 'You will have
to take her place, eh?'

'You mean—be a sort of daughter?'

'Why not?' A smile just touched his lips.

'But—you aren't a fatherly sort of person,
Jourdan.'

'I expect not.' He shrugged his shoulder. 'But I
shall get a lot of satisfaction out of knowing that
you aren't wheeling meal trolleys to the sick;
instead you can explore the island and recapture
some of your own childhood. It's a pity Jody will
not be your playmate, but you don't mind being
on your own too much, eh?'

'No, I don't mind.'

'You are a loner at heart, is that it, Melly?'

'I—I suppose I find it protective,' she admitted. 'My grandmother and I were very close and I suppose I put up a kind of barrier when she was gone and I had no one to go home to any more. We shared so much—she was so young at heart and I hardly bothered to make friends of my own age——'

She broke off, fighting the sudden tears that threatened to overspill. She had learned to control her emotions and it was more than ever essential that she control them in front of Jourdan.

'Never mind, you and I will be friends,' he said. 'I realise that is what you want and need.'

She nodded, and it came as relief when the request that they fasten their seat-belts flashed on.

Within a short time of landing they were on their way to the plantation house. Their cab drove along a narrow coastal road that grew steep and twisting so that sometimes they seemed to hover in mid-air before plunging on to solid ground again. Their driver seemed oblivious of any danger and they sped along through the bright sunlight, the wheel twisting and turning in the big brown hands.

Far below the road the sea glittered like hot silver under the assault of the afternoon sun, but it didn't seem any cooler when they drove inland among great clumps of greenery where flickers of scarlet could be seen. These were the fiery petals of flame-of-the-forest, Jourdan told her, and Melly noticed that he looked alert and challenging, as if he was intent on overcoming his disappointment where Jody was concerned.

The island teemed with gorgeous flowers and he named them for Melly, indicating the hibiscus, heady-scented magnolias, cascading wisterias and dazzling zinnias. At night from the heart of the plantation she would hear many sounds, she was told, that would seem strange at first and perhaps disturbing. There would be the rattling sound of the wind in the huge banana leaves and she might also hear the peacocks, for they wandered there at night.

'Quite soon you will begin to feel like an islander,' Jourdan assured her. 'You will never want to live anywhere else but at Bel-Aze.'

Melly was a little doubtful about the heat; her skin and hair felt so moist that she could feel the strength seeping out of her pores, leaving her limp.

'I could do with a cup of tea,' she said longingly.

'We are almost home,' Jourdan consoled her. 'Soon you will get your cup of tea and a cool shower. The heat is trying at first, but your system will adjust to it. You must eat plenty of fruit, and there is no shortage of delicious fruit on Bel-Aze. The pineapples are luscious and Bethula makes a tasty punch from the juice to which she adds just a dash of rum and spice. Wait until you taste it!'

Soon the cab turned off the road and bumped along a shady track where the trees seemed to be woven together so that it was like driving along a tunnel. The sudden dimness and coolness was welcome and they went on for more than a mile; it wasn't a straight path but one that gradually curved as if winding around the estate that Jourdan owned. Stabs of sunlight began to filter down as gaps widened in the weaving of trees and moments later they drove between a pair of stone posts into a palm court where the cab came to a stop.

'We are home!' There was a note of pleasure in Jourdan's voice and the look of strain had vanished from his face.

As they climbed from the cab a woman came down the steps of the wide verandah which completely encompassed this sprawling house which had a deeply thatched roof in a burned-gold colour. 'Here you are, boss, home at last!' The woman who came to greet them was ample and warm-coloured, with a rich laugh. 'Tea is ready laid for the both of you.'

'Tea!' exclaimed Melly, with a catch of anticipation in her voice. 'I'm gasping for a cup!'

Bethula looked Melly up and down. 'Well, boss, there isn't a great deal of your little lady, and I almost took her for your little girl. Now where is that child? I understood she was coming with you?'

'She isn't, Bethula.' Jourdan turned from paying the cab driver, and the sound of the cab speeding away filled the silence that followed his words.

'Now what you mean by that?' Bethula demanded. 'You wrote to tell me to get her room all ready and nice——'

'Jody is staying on with her mother,' he explained. 'She now has a stepfather and I decided not to unsettle her, not at the present time. If she ever writes to say she's unhappy, then that will change matters and I shall go and fetch her without any hesitation.'

'And so I should think.' Bethula regarded

Melly. 'Perhaps, boss, it won't be too long before that nice little room can be used—seems a shame to have it standing empty.'

Her implication was obvious ... Jourdan was newly married and it was Melly's business to provide him with a child if he wanted one. 'I—I do like your house, Jourdan,' she said hastily. 'I love thatched roofs—Gran's cottage was thatched and it always looked a picture in the springtime when all the flowers were coming into bloom and the sun reflected in the tiny glass windows. I wished I had a painting of it.'

'Why not take up painting now you have the time for it?' Jourdan suggested. 'We shall have to discuss it, eh?'

Bethula stood looking at the two of them as if astounded by such a conversation from a newly married couple. She seemed to be wondering why Jourdan's arm wasn't wrapped around Melly's waist, and when Jourdan saw the look of perplexity on her face he broke into a smile.

'Melly has been a very hard-working girl,' he explained, 'and I owe her my life. We share a rare type of blood and when I suffered my ruptured appendix she was able to supply the transfusion that I badly needed. You and I, Bethula, are going to take good care of her.'

Bethula showed her fine white teeth in a broad smile, as if this remark from Jourdan was more in keeping with her idea of how a brand new husband should behave. 'I hope, Miss Melly, you aren't the sort that likes to live on celery sticks and cottage cheese, because I like to cook, and the boss will tell you I cook real good.'

Jourdan slanted a smile at Melly. 'Bethula

believes in a man having plenty of armful of woman!'

Melly felt her heart skip a beat, for it was only to be expected that Bethula looked upon them as a couple who had married so they could enjoy the pleasures of the matrimonial state. 'I've been told you're the best cook on the island,' she said quickly, 'but right now I'm longing for a cup of tea.'

Tall trees shaded the house which had a glory of bougainvillaea tumbling down from the golden crust of a roof, bright vermilion and deep violet, and as Melly mounted the steps into the verandah she realised that it must be twelve feet in width and spacious as an outside room. Underfoot the floor was tiled and there were tall wooden columns smothered in vines and lamps were attached to the walls. Long chairs in curled rattan were set about, low tables alongside them. It all looked very inviting, and because the verandah roof was so wide it was well shaded.

Jourdan touched a hand to her waist. 'What do you think of your new home, Melly? Does it meet with your approval?'

She turned to look up at him and felt again that dazzle of shock induced by the sheen of his eyes in his teak-brown face. She wanted to catch hold of his arm and press close to his big frame, but instead she had to hold in her feelings.

'It's like a picture postcard,' she said warmly. 'It's beautiful!'

'You seem a little surprised.' He arched an eyebrow. 'Were you expecting something a little more backwoods?'

Bethula gave a laugh that was rich and bubbling as warm brown sugar, and when they

entered the house there was coolness from big
fans whirling their blades in the high white-
painted ceilings. Here the floors were of a deep
rich timber and there was an air of spaciousness,
and Melly realised that all the rooms were on one
level and there were great sprays of tropical lilies
in big vases.

She was ushered into the room where tea was
laid and again there was a purring of ceiling fans
and a cool spaciousness so the air could circulate.
The walls were walnut-panelled, giving a golden
effect, and Melly noticed a deep recess crammed
with books, where a deep leather chair resided.

'This is so—so nice!' She stood absorbing into
herself the atmosphere of this house in which she
was to live with Jourdan, far from the maddening
crowds of London, entirely removed from the
grimy bricks and glass of the city where the
traffic was unceasing.

Her gaze focused on a round table with a pair
of chairs beside it, teapot and cups grouped on a
lace cloth, sandwiches and home-made cakes
arranged on plates.

This was home on the island of Bel-Aze and
here, she hoped, she might find a degree of
happiness with the husband to whom she must be
a proxy daughter rather than a wife.

Jourdan watched her as he stood lighting a
cheroot and Melly wondered if the same thoughts
were going through his mind. She gave a little
sigh and sank down on the rattan-framed couch.

'You're travel tired, girl, and a nice cup of tea
will set you up again.' Bethula bustled to the
table and began to pour the tea.

Melly relaxed against a cushion and felt her
body growing less tense; the left side of her ached

a little and she gave her arm a rub. How strong the scent of the tropical lilies, as if their silken trumpets blew out the perfume like a silent music.

'That was the arm you knocked—does it still bother you?' Jourdan narrowed his eyes at her through the smoke of his cheroot.

'The bruise itches,' she said lightly. 'Thank you, Bethula.' She buried her nose in her teacup and savoured the pleasure of her tea.

'Is that the way you like it, Miss Melly?'

'Perfect bliss, Bethula, and I would love one of those cakes with the wings and all that lovely cream.'

'Angel kisses.' Bethula placed two on a plate along with a couple of sandwiches. 'Now you eat good and get yourself cuddlesome for that big man. You eat some of my cakes as well, boss. Smoking is the devil's work!'

'I daresay it is, Bethula.' And with a shameless smile through the smoke he watched his housekeeper bustle out of the room. 'That good soul of a woman keeps a layabout of a husband who won't do a stroke of work. The dictates of the heart might be the devil's work at times.'

Melly gave him a quick look and caught a sombre expression on his face. She decided that he was thinking about Irene and the way his life had been bedevilled by her. 'Do have some tea, Jourdan. Shall I pour out for you?'

'If you would be so kind.'

Melly poured out with her right hand but made the mistake of reaching for the sugar bowl with her left hand ... suddenly as sometimes happened her fingers weakened and the bowl tipped its contents over the table. 'Oh—dammit!'

As she scooped the sugar back into the bowl she felt Jourdan's eyes intent upon her.

'Are you certain that arm is all right, Melly? You did give it a nasty crack that evening on the ship and the bruise was a bad one. Hold out your arm and let me check again that you haven't damaged the bone.'

'I'm just clumsy,' she said airly. 'There, that's most of the sugar back in the bowl——'

But he was looming over her and with an insistent hand he took her arm in his fingers, unbuttoned the cuff of her sleeve and pushed the silk above her elbow so he could study her forearm. The bruise was fading but was still evident there against her sensitive skin, and tiny nerves contracted deep inside Melly when Jourdan moved his fingers over the bruised area.

'Does it hurt when I touch you?' he asked.

Speaking might have betrayed the tremor that was running through her so she shook her head.

'Are you absolutely sure, *mignonne*?'

She nodded.

'You would tell me the truth?' He was frowning down at her. 'I have noticed more than once that your arm seems a little weak at times. Why is that?'

'Oh, I had a riding fall a long time ago, when I was quite young, and my arm troubles me now and then.' She couldn't quite meet his eyes and her lashes flickered. 'I'm not made of glass, Jourdan. I'm really quite a tough country girl.'

'Tough is hardly the word I would use.' He drew down her sleeve and buttoned the cuff. 'I used to do this for Jody when she was small . . . the devil take that mother of hers! We could have had a merry time, the three of us!'

Brows drawn together, he carried his cup of tea to his deep leather chair and sat there with a brooding air. Melly nibbled a cake and felt troubled for him. All his plans had involved Jody and he was bound to feel disgruntled.

'I—I'm glad you've a nice lot of books,' she said. 'I enjoy a good read, so I hope they aren't all about war and adventure.'

'A lot of them are,' he admitted, 'but we can always arrange for Hatchard's to send out the sort of books you enjoy. Which authors do you like to read?'

'I like mystery writers.' She licked cream from her finger. 'I suppose you thought I was going to say I'm a Florence Del Rue fan?'

'Who on this earth is Florence Del Rue?'

'She writes about passion in the desert mostly, though some of her heroines fall for bullfighters and highland lairds.'

'Sounds monstrous, and how do you happen to know the contents of these silly books if you don't read them?'

'A lot of woman patients read them and sometimes I used to wheel the book trolley round the clinic. Florence Del Rue was high on the wanted list.'

'No doubt a good substitute for sleeping pills,' he said crisply. 'Make out your own list and I'll send it off to Hatchard's and arrange to have a nice fat parcel of mysteries delivered by airmail. You would like that, Melly?'

'Very much.' She gave him a smile of pleasure, lounging there with his long legs stretched across the floor, his eyes glinting beyond the shadow of his lashes. It was a look which she found partly fascinating and just a little frightening, for there was something of interrogation in it.

She bit into another cake. 'Jody would have loved these, wouldn't she? They're delicious.'

'Who was it who hurt you, Melly?' he demanded suddenly.

Her heart gave an uncomfortable throb. 'No one——'

'I'm determined to be told.' He leaned forward and his jaw had a menacing look. 'I want to know what you are bottling up inside you so that now and then I see a kind of terror in your eyes—especially when I happen to come near you. Why do I frighten you?'

'I—I don't have to tell you anything I don't want to——'

'You know of my past, so is it not reasonable that I should enquire about yours? You make me curious, and I wonder why a girl with a kind heart should surround it with a hedge of thorns.'

'It's my nature.' She tried to sound flippant. 'If you've a soft heart then it's wise to keep it protected.'

'From me?'

As the question slid from his lips Melly felt driven to her feet. 'I didn't come to Bel-Aze to be bullied by you—don't take your anger over Jody out on me! I can't help it that Irene altered all your plans and got you landed with a wife you don't really want! I won't put up with this—I'd sooner go back to England!'

She ran to the door and he instantly pursued her, catching her by the shoulders and swinging her around to face him. She had known that his reflexes were swift and dangerous, and in running away from him she had run straight into his arms.

'Please don't do this to me.' Tears welled into her eyes, dredged from memories she couldn't share with him. 'I can't stay here if you're going to—to hound me. It isn't fair when you said—said my life would be my own. That's what we promised each other, didn't we?'

His eyes scoured her tear-wet face. His hands tightened upon her shoulders and he propelled her towards him until they touched. 'I'm not using you to slake my anger with Irene. I think I knew all along that she would have things her way; she is that kind of woman. But you, Melly, you are so much her opposite that I feel I have the right to share whatever it is that puts that terrorised look in your eyes. It's as if you live with some appalling secret that actually gives you physical pain.'

His eyes swept over her, probing her with their steel. It was more than she could tolerate and she tore desperately free of his hands, backing away from him like a young animal at bay. 'I only married you,' she said, 'because you swore you wouldn't touch me. Wild horses wouldn't have dragged me to that Embassy to be married to you if I'd known you'd break your word. I trusted you, Jourdan. I listened to your story about your daughter and I wanted to help you because you seemed genuine. Now—now I don't know what to believe, and I think it might be best if I go home to England. You can get an annulment easy enough. Our marriage is only on paper.'

'In the name of heaven!' His gesture was very Gallic. 'What do I make of you, Melly? All I am trying to do is to understand your fears and you look at me as if I only intend to arouse them!'

Her eyes met his, braving them even as she

quaked inside. It wasn't fear of him she felt so much as fear of herself. He was never going to know that she was fighting her own feelings with all her strength.

'*Mignonne*, I don't want you to go back to England.' He thrust a hand through his hair. 'I don't like to hear you say that you don't trust me—I haven't brought you to Bel-Aze just to see you leave me. Come, be reasonable.'

'If you'll be the same, Jourdan,' she said quietly. 'It isn't much to ask, that you let me be the girl I am; the girl who came into your room at the clinic and was pleased you were alive because she had been able to help you. I don't ask for much, do I?'

'Ah, Melly,' he winced as if her words had touched a nerve, 'I know you don't ask for much, and that is what troubles me. No doubt I compare you to Irene. She demanded more than she was worth—very well, *mon bébé*, you get your way. If there are things you don't wish to tell me, then so be it. I shall respect your wishes.'

'Thank you, Jourdan.'

She had to be reassured by what he said, but that reassurance was rather shaken when she found that Bethula had put her into a bedroom with a connecting door into Jourdan's room. It was perfectly natural for his housekeeper to do this, and it would have seemed highly unnatural had Melly asked to be moved to a bedroom which didn't adjoin her husband's.

Melly accepted the arrangement for Jourdan's sake, realising that the island people might be inquisitive and likely to gossip if it became known that she and Jourdan weren't a normal couple who had an intimate relationship. A husband

and wife who roamed from room to room, at ease
with each other and in love.

It was a very attractive bedroom, with
furniture in ivory bamboo, a sprigged and pleated
canopy above the double bed where yards of
filmy muslin were looped back, ready to be
released at night so the occupants of the bed
could sleep undisturbed by winged and crawling
interlopers.

Melly stood gazing around her, taking in the
vanity table with a cane-seated stool, a cushioned
cane armchair, and bedlinen in pale peach with
broderie anglaise trim. A reflective look stole into
her eyes. Jourdan had referred to his home as a
bachelor establishment, yet this bedroom was
feminine in every detail.

Was it possible that this had been Irene's
bedroom? Melly walked across to the clothes
closet and slid open the louvred doors; the closet
was quite empty, but there was a lingering hint of
a seductive perfume . . . the kind of scent which a
fashionable woman would spray extravagantly on
her skin and her clothing.

Melly had to accept that Irene had been an
intimate part of Jourdan's life for a number of
years; someone quite different from herself. A
brunette, perhaps, in contrast to her own fairness.
Tall and svelte to match her air of self-
assurance, with a look in her eyes that told
everyone she thought well of herself.

Melly walked slowly to the vanity table and
gave herself a long, serious look in the mirror.
Slots of sunshine came into the room from the
half-closed shutters and her hair glistened where
the sun caught it. Yes, she decided, she was
undoubtedly as different from Irene as chalk

from cheese. Feeling the way he did about his ex-wife, Jourdan would never have married her likeness.

Turning from the mirror, Melly rested her gaze on the door leading to Jourdan's room. She placed her hand against her left side and she could feel the disturbing thump of her heart against her rib-cage. It was the strangest feeling, almost as if she were holding her heart in her hand.

Abruptly that adjoining door opened and Jourdan stood in the aperture gazing across at her ... beneath her fingers Melly felt the quickening of her heart. How tall he looked, and how very dark in contrast to the ivory and peach of this room ... a room which must hold for him memories of an intimate kind.

She had to say something ... anything that would shatter the silent intimacy of his thoughts. 'I was wondering—did Irene sleep here?'

He drew in his breath and plunged his hands into the pockets of his trousers. He had removed his jacket and tie, so his shirt looked very white against his brown skin.

'Do you mind?' he asked, in a tone of voice which suggested that she would be wasting her time if she did mind.

She shook her head. Any undue show of emotion would imply that she was jealous of Irene and she didn't want that idea to get into his head. 'It's such an attractive room that I guessed she used to sleep here. I can smell her perfume and I can imagine her sitting in front of the mirror, stroking a comb through her long dark hair.'

'How did you know she had long dark hair?' His eyes narrowed, pinning Melly to their steel.

'Intuition.' Melly's hand slid to her hip-bone, where it clenched. 'Irene gave you a hard time, so you wouldn't be likely to marry someone who resembled her, especially the way things are.'

'Between us, do you mean?' His voice matched the steely hardness of his gaze.

'Yes.' Her fingernails were digging into her palm. 'You were in love with Irene, but you had a different motivation for marrying me. I qualified because I didn't look anything like her.'

'You are so right about that, Melly.' There was a cutting edge to his voice. 'From top to toe there isn't a thing about you that reminds me of Irene. Her hair is as dusky as yours is fair. Her dark eyes could conceal a thousand secrets. She talks and walks as if she is melting with sensuality, but as men get older and wiser they learn that what is displayed on the cover is not always what is inside the book.'

As he said this Jourdan stepped into the room where his former wife had displayed her physical charms and disillusioned him with her vanity and self-engrossment.

Melly strove to stand perfectly still . . . not by a single movement would she betray how unnerved he made her as he came to where she stood, his eyes roving about the room as if remembering the last time he had shared it with Irene.

'Yes,' he said, 'there she would sit combing her hair, seeing in that mirror all that she wished to see. She would lean close to the glass and peer intently at her face, scanning it for the faintest line, the merest suspicion of a sag in her jawline. She would spend hours creaming her skin . . . the smallest blemish and she would become hysterical. That is what I endured from that silly vain woman, and you can stop looking at me as if wondering if she broke my heart! What broke me was that I lost Jody.'

At the slight break in his voice Melly's resolve almost broke ... she knew he was seeking to be consoled, but she was not the person to give him that consolation. The terms of their marriage had to be kept as they were, for that was the only way she could stay married to him.

'Jourdan, I can't say how sorry I am that your plans have misfired.' She stood there straight and slim, her eyes at their most reserved. 'But you still have the plantation and you said there's a lot to be done before it can become productive.'

'Indeed.' He spoke drily. 'It has been abominably neglected and needs a devil of a lot of work. Work which should so occupy me that I'm unlikely to have ideas about occupying myself with a reluctant bride—if that is on your mind?'

'No——'

He gestured at the adjoining room. 'I shall keep to my territory, but the door stays unlocked between us. I don't wish Bethula to become too curious about us—understood?'

'Yes.' Melly gave him a quick, faintly appealing look. 'Don't dislike me, Jourdan.'

'*Mon Dieu*, it isn't a question of dislike! The islanders are warm-natured and down-to-earth, and they wouldn't understand a marriage such as ours.'

Melly felt stricken for both of them, two people bound by the most tenuous bonds, agreeing to stay together because they had nothing better to do. 'You said you didn't want me to leave, but I'm prepared to go tomorrow. It's for you to say.'

'Stay,' he said morosely, 'but don't get bored.'

'Bored?' she exclaimed. 'I'm thinking of you— you married me for the best of reasons, and now there isn't a single reason why you should go on being married to me. If you have regrets, who can blame you?'

'We both know where to lay the blame.' He dragged a hand over his face as if trying to ease the muscles. 'This abrasive mood I'm in is due to Irene, not you—as soon as your furniture arrives from England it can replace all these items that relate to her. Every damned stick in this room can go up in smoke. A good blazing fire might exorcise some of her devilry!'

He swung on his heel and a moment later the door of his room clashed shut behind him. Melly stood with his words echoing through her mind . . . yes, with a kind of devilment Jody's mother had wrecked his chance of being a father to his own daughter, and now he must live with the knowledge that another man had replaced him in Jody's life.

With a flash of rage Melly turned to the vanity table, snatched up her atomiser and sprayed it all around the bedroom, banishing the scent of the selfish woman who had killed the love which Jourdan had felt for her. Not content with that she had found a way to rob him of his child, and Melly knew that it was essential in the days to come that he absorb himself in the rehabilitation of the banana groves. Hard work and ambition were the best tonic for abrased feelings.

Her first task in the morning was to find some other use for the little room Bethula had mentioned; the one she had prepared for Jody. It wasn't that Melly wanted Jourdan to forget the child, she didn't want him to remember what Bethula had said upon learning that Jody wasn't going to occupy the room.

With every good intention she had implied that it was Melly's duty to provide Jourdan with a child to take Jody's place. But for Melly it wasn't a simple, practical solution . . . it filled her with secret dread.

CHAPTER SEVEN

JOURDAN began the task of clearing the banana plantation the week they came home. He told Melly it was fearfully overgrown and he hired several men to help with the formidable task. They used long sugar-cane knives, chopping and stripping and weeding out the tropical tangles of snake-vine that stunted the growth of the banana palms.

The men sweated away for hours at a time and came wearily up into the verandah to take deep gulps of the cooling drinks Bethula made for them.

After a while Melly began to feel rather in the way, for there was very little she could do to help, and in the clearing process one of the men uncovered a nest of big spiders and Jourdan had them netted and drove with them into the forest beyond his land, where he released them. He sardonically informed Melly that he wanted to thrive, so his motto was to let the spiders run alive.

'How can you bear to touch them?' she asked, shuddering at the very thought. She adored animals and could tolerate most forms of insect life, but there was something about the leggy swiftness of spiders that made her skin creep.

'What a child you are!' Jourdan mocked. 'They are harmless enough, but I imagine it's the look of them you don't like.'

'I wouldn't mind if they didn't jump,' she

explained, and decided that while the clearing went on she would spend time down on the beach, which was reached by a rugged pathway that led down to the strand of white-gold sand below the rear of the plantation house.

Bethula gave her a pack of sandwiches along with a flask of fruit juice, and wearing a brimmed straw hat, shirt and shorts, Melly would set off feeling jaunty and carefree, a copy of Sherlock Holmes stories tucked beneath her arm.

She revelled in the isolation of the beach and strove not to look too far into the future. Each day the sun shone bright as gold and the warm feel of it on her skin had a healing power all its own. It stroked away her cares as it warmly stroked her skin, until in a while she began to resemble a gently tanned urchin who paddled in the rock pools and discovered seashells whose markings so delighted her that she found herself carrying them home.

The plantation had become her home, and how different each day was from waking up to a rain-wet morning in London, knowing that the buses would be overcrowded, with everyone pushing and grabbing for handrails, their overcoats giving off that tang of damp wool. And ten to one on a wet, grey morning someone at the clinic would be in a grumpy mood and there would be a chain reaction of irritability.

But when Melly wended her way down the path to the beach it was as if she were on holiday. She didn't need to worry about pleasing anyone but herself. Shards of sun-gold fell through the interlaced branches and slid warm down her arms and legs, and she loved the way the sea glinted like silver foil.

There were sea-carved boulders that offered shade when the sun really began to beat the sands. The great slabs of rock stood boldly against the blue blending of ocean and sky. She would recline there on the pale, velvety sand, bemused by her own idleness, for there had been few times in Melly's life when she had been free to enjoy a life of leisure. She took pleasure in the sea breezes fingering her hair and was amused by the hermit crabs that turned over the sea-wrack, comically clad in cast-off shells. She told Jourdan they looked like little old women at jumble sales turning over cast off hats and coats.

He smiled in the lazy way he had, and yet with a questing light at the centres of his eyes as he sat with her on the verandah at sundown, he with a rum cocktail on the table beside his long chair, she with a tall glass of fruit juice garnished with pineapple, lime and tangerine. Jourdan would study her in his rather disturbing way and tell her that each day she looked more tanned so that her hair was fairer than ever.

'Do I take it that you sunbathe down there on the sands?' he asked. 'Taking your ease like a lady of leisure while I sweat in the groves like a coolie!'

'You know you enjoy it,' she replied, tinkling the ice in her glass. 'You're the boss, the master of all you survey.'

'Including you, Melly?'

'Including everything on your territory, I should think.' She drank from her glass so she wouldn't have to look at him directly; as always he unnerved her when he grew personal.

'Do you consider me an arrogant man?' he wanted to know.

'Isn't arrogance built into every man?' she retaliated, her heart quickened by the way he looked in a tropic white jacket, his shirt open-necked to show his skin tanned to mahogany. With the black sweep of hair above his eyes he had a look that attacked Melly's innermost feelings . . . emotions she had to conceal with an assumed air of coolness.

'I wonder if you would prefer me to be the tweed-clad, pipe-smoking type of husband. Would you?'

'So I could fit into that father-and-daughter relationship you spoke about, Jourdan? Is that what you mean?' The wide-eyed look she gave him was innocent enough, but in reality she knew what lay at the root of his remark. He believed that if he was a more comfortable type of man, then she might be more at ease with him.

'I wonder if that is what I mean?' He slanted a lazy smile at Bethula as she came out to tell them dinner was ready. They went indoors to eat steamed butterfish with melon and shrimp, followed by crisp lamb cutlets with sweet potatoes and peas. Dessert was a delicious deep damson pie served with cream. Coffee was brought to them in the den, where they settled down to listen to a James Last concert on the radio.

'I hope you don't miss those plush London cinemas?' Jourdan remarked, deep in his leather chair, eyes screened by his cheroot smoke. 'I know how much you enjoyed your Saturday evening visit to the flicks . . . tell me, *mon enfant*, did you never go there with a young man? Did you always buy your own peanuts and tub of ice-cream? Did you never long for a romance of your very own?'

'Real life romance is never the way it is in films,' she said lightly. 'Did any man ever look at a woman the way Robert Redford does?'

'Is he your ideal?' Jourdan drawled.

'Of course,' she smiled. 'I'm mad about his blue eyes.'

'Mad about him so long as he stays up there on the movie screen, eh?'

She nodded, quite certain that torture wouldn't have dragged from her the truth of her feelings, that in her eyes Jourdan was far more fascinating then any movie star she had ever sat and watched.

They retired to bed fairly early, for Jourdan spent from sunrise to sundown in the plantation groves and it was tiring work. As Melly prepared for bed she could hear him moving about in his own room; before getting into bed he would open her door and wish her a good night's sleep, and she always made certain she was deep in the cane armchair with a book, her robe covering her nightdress.

Jourdan never lingered. He respected her wish in the matter of bedroom privacy and she made no attempt to divine his feelings, whether it amused or annoyed him when he looked in to find her with her nose in a book. Before closing the connecting door he would drily advise her not to strain her eyes, possibly aware that it was her nerves that were under strain when he stood there in his black robe, his hair damp and tousled from his shower.

Not until he was gone, the door closed between them, could she relax. Then she would sit quietly there and catch the drifting scent of his cheroot,

an image of him printed dark and strong upon
her mind. Their marriage was not the usual sort,
but their blood had mingled and Melly felt close
to him in spirit, as if some part of her drifted to
him and lay close against his heart.

Their days blended together into a pattern
which had its own harmony. No one came to
disturb Melly's hours on the beach, where she lay
alone on sands laced with a frill of surf.
Sometimes there were black sea-eggs on the
beach and she had been warned to avoid them,
because their spikes could pierce a foot and cause
a painful infection. A far more welcome visitor
was the rosy flamingo, strutting on stilt legs in
the surf and quite unconcerned by the quiet girl
in the big straw hat.

The sea breezes rustled the leaves of the tamarisk
and the deep green fans of the palms, and if now
and again it crossed Melly's mind that her Eden
must have its serpent, she thrust away the thought
and went hunting for shells and pieces of driftwood
which the sea had carved into fanciful shapes.

In order to avoid the spiny sea-eggs she wore a
pair of paddling shoes which Bethula had found
in a cupboard. It was while she was trying them
on that Melly had asked if Irene came often to
the plantation house to be with Jourdan before
the break-up of their marriage.

'She come when it suit her,' Bethula replied,
and it was unusual to see her warm brown face
without its smile. 'That last time she came to
spend a leave with the boss, seems to me they
were trying to save what was left of their
marriage. But she was aggravating him all the
time, bored with being so far from town and
wanting to go dancing and socialising.'

Bethula shook her head as she recalled for Melly the details of that final leave which Jourdan had spent with Irene. 'There was the boss needing some relaxation after a rather tough mission, and that selfish woman of his didn't want to give him anything but the sharp edge of her tongue, and it could be razor-sharp when she chose! Then early one morning a cab came to the house and she went off alone. Mr Jourdan didn't try to stop her. Things were over between them, and a few months later their divorce was settled and she got custody of the child because he was a serviceman.'

A deep sigh escaped Bethula and she cast a rather speculative look at Melly. 'Looks like he'll never get to have his Jody with him!'

It was a remark that lingered in Melly's mind. She knew very well what lay behind such hints ... she was Jourdan's new wife, so what was stopping her from providing Jourdan with a child to take the place of Jody?

Melly knelt on the beach rubbing a crust of sand from a ribbed shell, but her gaze was on the far-out lash and foam of the sea as it flung itself at the reef, roaring in a kind of frustration, hissing as the waves broke on the spine of coral and slithered away.

Sometimes her own emotions felt as torn and restless as those waves, up against a barrier that had to be as firm and wounding as the coral. She had known this from the very beginning and perhaps she should have told Jourdan why it was wrong for them to marry, but he had swept away her doubts and assured her that it wouldn't matter that their marriage would never be a real one.

Melly reclined on the sand like a lonely, stranded starfish, the surf lapping at her outstretched legs. A marriage of convenience could survive if it didn't receive a jolt such as the one Irene had provided by her marriage to a man who had taken Jody under his wing. Denied one daughter, Jourdan might desire another to take Jody's place, and if that happened then he would look at Melly in a new light ... one that she couldn't face.

Troubled by her secret fears as she was, it didn't really concern her the day Chantal André drove a sleek car between the gateposts of the plantation house and with a whip of the wheels drew it to a standstill at the foot of the verandah steps.

Melly sat there enjoying a slice of melon and she watched as the female driver of the sports car slid from behind the wheel and revealed herself as fashionably slim and very chic in a soft silk dress with a deep neck plunge. A sleek swathe of red-brown hair concealed an elegant profile and her shoes had jade-green heels that gleamed in the sun like lizard-skin. Above her left ankle, beneath sheer hose, there was a glint of a golden chain.

She came up the verandah steps to where Melly sat and there was a poise and sway to her walk of a woman who liked to be watched; someone who might be a model or an actress. Undoubtedly a person who was very sure of her own attractions.

'So you are the new wife of Jourdan, *vraiment*?' Her voice was throaty and tinged with a silky malice which Melly's look of simplicity seemed to induce in women of dedicated artificiality.

'Yes, I'm Mrs Lanier.' Melly had not long climbed the path from the beach and was aware that her hair was untidy, that there was sand on her legs and a rip in her shirt where she had caught it on a shrub.

'For one moment I thought you might be his daughter.' The unexpected visitor slid her eyes over Melly and they didn't miss a detail of her face and figure. 'But then I remembered that he had told me she has his own colouring—may I say that you have a clever *coiffeur*, that he or she is able to so lighten your hair that the roots show no darkness.'

'I never visit a hairdresser.' Melly could feel a stiffening of her spine; a prickling of her skin that warned her this woman was no casual acquaintance of Jourdan's. 'You are a friend of my husband's?'

'*Voilà*, I come bearing a gift for you both.' A wrapped package was placed on the cane table in front of Melly. 'A shaker for cocktails—you do drink them, eh? Or is your preference for watermelon?'

'I quite like both.' Melly didn't lay a finger on the package; the Frenchwoman was obviously a friend of Jourdan's, so he could open it and admire the contents. 'Won't you sit down? And would you like a drink?'

There was a pitcher of lemonade on the table and with an air of innocence Melly filled a glass to the brim with the innocuous mineral. As the elegant visitor sank down into one of the cane chairs, the silky dress emitted the fragrance of a sophisticated perfume.

'My name is Chantal André.' She eyed the glass of lemonade with a dubious air. 'Jourdan might have mentioned me to you?'

'He may have done.' The implication, as Melly well knew, was that Jourdan was unlikely to have mentioned an old girl-friend to a very new wife. 'I haven't met many of his friends, and he's been so busy getting the banana groves in order that by sundown all he wants to do is relax here on the verandah.'

'So he intends to remain on the island—you are not just honeymooning?' Chantal took a sip of the lemonade and the look she gave Melly implied that she thought her as insipid as the pale, cool drink.

'Jourdan's very keen to get the groves in working order.' Melly pushed the melon rind away from her and wiped her lips, and she knew from the way Chantal raised a hair-fine eyebrow that she thought Jourdan's bride gauche and quite without the chic that Frenchmen were supposed to demand in their women. 'He's quite determined to become a successful planter here on Bel-Aze.'

'You are telling me that Jourdan has left the Service?'

'Yes, when we married.'

'At your request, may one ask?' Chantal spoke as if she had possessed certain rights over Jourdan.

'It was entirely his own idea—as you probably know, Miss André, no one tells Jourdan what to do. He's entirely his own master.'

'And yours?' The words slid silkily from the expertly painted lips.

'He's bigger than me, so I don't argue,' Melly said lightly.

'You are much younger than he, so that, perhaps, is why you assume that the man must be the master.'

'I don't see why the one with the muscles shouldn't carry the weight of the decisions.' Melly smiled as she spoke, her unpainted face framed by the light-gold hair, a tinge of amusement filtering in and out of her sherry-coloured eyes. Not pretty, but there was something haunting in her look that other girls had to shade into their looks with the aid of a cosmetic.

'How *démodée* you are!' Chantal gave her a rather patronising look. 'How did Jourdan ever come to meet you, let alone marry you? That *monstre sacré* knew I was waiting for him to propose to me—ah, you open wide the eyes, *chérie*, as if shocked that I should speak my feelings. Did you think that your masterful Jourdan denied himself—like a monk?'

'What Jourdan did before he married me has nothing to do with me,' Melly replied, but deep inside herself she felt a leap of resentment that this Frenchwoman should come here and make claims upon Jourdan; her manner insinuating that an unworldly wife could be pushed aside quite easily.

'You feel no jealousy—no displeasure that I come here to look you over?' Chantal narrowed her jade-green eyes, their colour reflecting the jade jewel clawed in gold that hung around her slim neck. The jade glowed darkly green there in the deep V of her neckline and Melly knew it would direct a man's attention to the alluring figure displayed by the water-lily silk.

'You must admire Jourdan with such a young and trusting love,' Chantal said inquisitively.

'Must I?' murmured Melly, for at the clinic she had learned to deal with self-possessed women such as this one and in exchange for guile she gave them her disconcerting candour.

'But of course.' Chantal gave a slightly forced laugh. 'You are the romantic type—one has only to look at you. You met Jourdan in England, eh?'

'In London. Jourdan had an operation and was a patient at the clinic where I was employed to help prepare and serve the meals.' Melly kept her gaze on Chantal's face and saw a flicker of disdain travel across her features. It didn't really surprise her that the Frenchwoman had attracted Jourdan; she had those attributes which had attracted him to Irene. The chic awareness of fashion, a svelte figure and one of those detailed faces that could look faintly cruel.

Jourdan's profession had been highly dangerous, and it seemed natural in Melly's view that he should be drawn to women like the one who faced her across the cane table, a wing of red-brown hair casually draped against the sculptured cheekbone.

Slowly Chantal raised an eyebrow. 'You worked as a maid! *Chérie*, that is truly astonishing!'

'People have to eat,' Melly smiled. 'I don't call that astonishing.'

'You know very well what I mean, that you are so opposite to Jourdan's first wife.' Chantal stroked a fingertip down the line of her jaw, as if she never ceased to enjoy the pleasure of being a good-looking woman. 'Irene was so well connected, so chic and self-assured.'

'Oh, I'm well aware that I'm none of those things.' Though Melly still smiled, her eyes had a faraway look in them. 'I have no connections at all, I'm a casual dresser and I have very little vanity. Perhaps Jourdan required a change of scenery.'

Chantal's eyes narrowed to a glittering green. 'He always had an ironic sense of humour,' she drawled.

'Do you think that was his motive in marrying me?' asked Melly. 'You think I'm a joke he felt like playing on his—friends?'

The slightest of shrugs lifted the silk-clad shoulders. 'When I heard he was here with a brand new wife I naturally assumed—well, let us say, *chérie*, that it takes one by surprise to find that a man of the world has married a mere girl who seems not to know a lot about the world. You say you worked as a maid so how could you have learned?'

'Perhaps I was busy learning other things?' murmured Melly. 'Perhaps I wanted to do more than skate across the surface of life, being a bright butterfly rather than a caring person? When people talk about being people of the world they usually mean that they're busy collecting sensations; dipping their wings in the sunlight and making sure they avoid the shadows where someone might be in need of help.'

'*Mon Dieu*,' Chantal widened her eyes, 'you are unbelievable! Have you so reformed Jourdan with your saintly ideas that I shan't recognise any more the exciting man I used to know so well?'

Melly didn't miss the way Chantal laid stress on those last few words. 'Have you known him a long time?' she asked, outwardly calm in the face of Chantal André, so self-aware and patronising, and unconcerned if her remarks maltreated the feelings of another woman. Only with men did her type switch on the seductive charm.

'On and off,' Chantal drawled, a note of meaning in her voice. 'I am *chanteuse* at the Café Zelle in town. I supply music and song to those who come to drink and dine there. Jourdan came often after his marriage went on the rocks. He was lonely and attractive and we became— friends.'

'That was nice for him,' commented Melly, a thread of irony in her voice. 'I know it saddened him that his broken marriage meant that he saw less of his daughter.'

'The child is still with her mother, eh? Did you not wish——?'

'Irene has remarried,' Melly broke in. 'I would have welcomed being friends with Jody, but it seems that Irene's new husband wants to be a father to Jourdan's daughter and he refuses to turn her into a tug-of-love child.'

'Always the *beau sabreur*.' Chantal snapped open her handbag and took from it a jewelled cigarette-case. 'Do you smoke?'

Melly shook her head.

'Have you no vices?' Chantal lit a cigarette, her lighter making a sharp little click. She expelled smoke from her nostrils and not for a second did she take her gaze from Melly's face. There was a kind of silken insolence about her, almost as if she had decided that Melly offered no real competition and she could win Jourdan back to her.

'What is one person's vice is another's accepted way of life,' Melly rejoined. 'Who am I to preach?'

'So you turn the other cheek, eh?'

Melly gazed directly back at Chantal, who smoked her cigarette with the same elegance with

which she wore her silk dress and implied that
Jourdan had been her lover . . . that if she wanted
him again as a lover, then Melly would have to
turn her cheek and endure the sting of it.

'The plantation house has an interesting
layout, *non*? The groves flanking it, and the beach
below—tell me, do you go swimming in the nude
with Jourdan?' Chantal's gaze drifted over
Melly's figure, taking the measure of her
youthfulness, her eyes resting on the slight bust
beneath the casual shirt. 'It was always something
he enjoyed and that solitary strip of beach is
convenient for nude bathing—and whatever else
takes his fancy.'

It was then, as Melly imagined Jourdan's hard
brown body stripped to this woman's gaze, that
she felt a stab of shocking resentment. It plunged
through her left side, like a knife-point against
skin and bone.

'As I told you, Jourdan's been so busy in the
groves that he hasn't found time for other
activities.' Melly pitched her voice to a low,
careful note, for she didn't want Chantal to guess
how much it hurt to hear of those intimate hours
down on the sands. 'I spend quite a bit of time
down on the beach; it makes a peaceful change
after the rush and roar of working in London.'

'You are not a Londoner, I think.' The jade
eyes probed Melly's face, sharp and green. 'You
seem to have a certain simplicity that seems not
of the city.'

'I was raised in the country—Devonshire.'

'Where the people are more God-fearing than
in cities, eh?' As Chantal raised her cigarette to
her lips the sun caught the gold serpent that
encircled her wrist, its tiny jade eyes seeming to

flicker. 'I was raised in Paris, the most civilised city in the world. Have you ever been there?'

'No, but Jourdan took me to New York.' It seemed to Melly that the serpent had glided into her garden of Eden in the slim and elegant shape of a woman she could never compete with in a physical sense. It seemed that she had to let happen what was inevitable when Jourdan met Chantal again. How could he not help remembering their good times together, especially down on the velvety sands where the gold-orange cliffs ensured privacy?

How could he not look at the Frenchwoman and compare her glamour and sensual beckoning with the cool restraint which Melly had shown him? Chantal was in every way the type of female to appeal to a vibrant male, and only for his daughter's sake had he returned to Bel-Aze a married man. Perhaps he had never thought of Chantal in relation to a child, whereas he had seen in Melly a companion for Jody, and that was all that mattered to him when he had proposed to her.

Melly felt quite certain that had Irene sent word to him in London that she had taken a second husband, the course of her own life wouldn't have changed and brought her to this tropical island. Right now she would be wheeling a meal trolley along the corridors of the clinic ... she wouldn't be sitting on the verandah of Jourdan's house, face to face with the woman he had turned to after his separation from Irene.

'Did you enjoy New York?' asked Chantal. 'You did not find it hectic and just a little alarming, a girl of the country as you are?'

'I thought it rather fantastic, especially at

night.' Melly remembered how she had stood with Jourdan on the balcony of their suite and gazed at the city's skyline as the sun sank down into the Hudson River, casting its boldly flaming glare into the countless windows of the tall buildings which were built on solid rock. Then night had fallen and chains of neon lights lay across the streets like a network of magic that concealed the throb of violence.

During those few days in New York it had been evident from the frequency of the wailing police sirens that the swift pace of modern life had quickened all kinds of passions in the veins of people living in the concrete jungle.

'It was an experience,' Melly said quietly, 'but I think I prefer Bel-Aze. I've never in my life seen such flowers and trees, and the other morning on the beach I saw a turtle with a shell like a medieval shield. Of course, some of the creatures are weird and alarming, especially the fiddler crab, with that large deformed claw that it uses to fight with. And the air in the evening is limpid as the touch of silk.'

'The island has its charm,' Chantal agreed, 'but Paris is beautiful. It has an ambience like no other in the world—one day I shall return.'

'What keeps you here?' Even as she spoke Melly caught the sound of free-striding steps across the palm court.

'Jourdan!' Chantal rose to greet him, the fluid silk of her dress showing the outlines of her figure. She broke into a spate of French as she went to him, hands outstretched.

Melly sat there and felt as if she were the visitor and Chantal the woman who waited eagerly for his return from his labours. As he

vaulted the verandah steps she was there and
clinging to him, to his hard frame clad in a
cambric shirt that clung to his moist brown skin.
She gazed up at him, at his hair clinging to his
forehead in damp strands . . . he looked as hard as
ironwood and just as dark, his skin baked by the
hot sun of the island.

'Chantal!' There was an unmistakable note of
pleasure in his voice, and Melly saw his hands
close on the silk-clad waist, warm and strong and
intimate. A little shiver ran through Melly; the
kind that jealousy produces.

'Yes, it is I, *mon diable*. You knew I was
awaiting only the word from you and you do this
to me!' She gestured carelessly at Melly. 'When
shall I catch you between wives, eh?'

Yet even as she spoke, calling him a devil, she
flung her arms about his neck, going up on the
toes of her green-heeled shoes so she could press
her lips to his. After several moments his hands
on her waist gently eased her away from him, as if
he had become aware of Melly's gaze upon him.

'Well, *enchanté de te voir, ma chérie*.'

'How dare you say you are delighted to see
me?' She pouted her lips and pressed against
him. 'Why have you not been to see me?'

'I have been busy, Chantal. Has my wife not
told you that I have been working like a mule in
my plantation?'

'She has told me something of the sort.'
Chantal cast a glance at Melly through a glossy
wing of hair. 'What a way to spend your
honeymoon, *mon cher*!'

'Melly's an understanding girl,' he rejoined.

'If a man said that about me, Jourdan, I would
throttle him.' Chantal closed her hands about

Jourdan's firm brown neck, the tips of her painted fingernails digging into his flesh. 'But she is *intimidée*, this young wife you have taken. She isn't what I expected.'

'I daresay you are surprised.' He lifted his hands and without effort released Chantal's hold on him. 'Have you had a drink?'

'I was given some lemonade.' Chantal wrinkled her nose. 'This Melly, she is so unwordly, *hein*? Where did you find her, I ask myself, when first I see her? Was it in a pet shop, or perhaps a nursery, but she tells me she worked as a hospital maid. Does she wait upon you, *mon cher*? Does she bring your slippers and light your cheroot?'

'No.' It was at Melly he frowned as he thrust his black hair back from his brow. Abruptly he looked displeased, raking his eyes over Melly's casually clad figure, then he turned to Chantal, as if her chic appearance pleased him more.

'You would like a daiquiri, eh? Are you staying to dinner? Has Melly invited you?'

'*Non.*' Chantal shook her head and pouted her red lips at him. 'Are you inviting me, *mon cher*?'

'If you are hungry.'

'But of a certainty I am hungry.' And Chantal managed to sound as if she was hungry for him. 'How fit you are looking, which must mean that you are quite recovered from your operation.'

'Quite recovered. It was nothing too serious.' He spoke curtly, and this brought Melly to her feet like a whiplash.

'I—I have to go and get ready for dinner— please excuse me.' Melly hastened indoors and left Jourdan to rediscover the fascinating Chantal, equipped as she was with a perfect figure, alluring green eyes, and confidence in her allurement.

It had started, Melly told herself as she went to her room. She had sensed that there had to be someone to whom Jourdan must turn for the excitement and ardour that was natural to his nature. She had believed she could accept it with equanimity, but it wasn't that easy. Perhaps if she liked Chantal André a little more, it might be possible to accept that Jourdan found her attractive.

But Melly didn't like Chantal. She didn't like her artificiality and the edge of malice to her tongue, and while standing beneath the shower Melly kept her gaze turned away from the wall mirror, her jaw clenched with a mixture of pain and temper.

The André woman was insolent and patronising; she was exactly the type Jourdan had labelled self-engrossed, yet he seemed drawn to the type as if he couldn't help himself. No doubt the attraction was physical, and slowly Melly turned to face the mirror so she could study her own figure with unsparing eyes.

There was no denying that Chantal André had a seductive figure, and Melly drew a sigh as she turned off the water and grabbed one of the big bath towels from the handrail. She enveloped herself in it, patting herself dry as she wandered into her bedroom.

Jourdan was standing there waiting for her, his darkness overwhelming in that setting of ivory bamboo and peach-coloured bedlinen that matched the curtains.

Melly caught her breath in consternation and tightened the folds of bath towel about her damp

body. She even retreated a step, as if half inclined
to escape back into the bathroom.

'Don't do that,' said Jourdan, dark brows
drawn together above his stern eyes. 'I have
something to say to you.'

'Can't it wait until I get dressed?' Her heart
was thumping beneath the towel that she
clutched around her, and she was unbearably
conscious of her bare shoulders, a scared look in
her eyes.

'I'm not stopping you from getting dressed.'
His frown was almost threatening. 'We can talk
while you dress.'

'No——' The word broke from her and she
couldn't keep the note of panic out of her voice.

'Why on earth not?' He swept his eyes over her
and they had the look of tempered steel. 'You try
my patience with your childish prudery, do you
know that, Melly?'

'Then—then go back to your mistress.' Colour
rushed into Melly's face. 'I shouldn't think she's
a prude!'

'Chantal is not my mistress,' he said angrily.

'I—I'm not a child, Jourdan.' Melly tilted her
chin. 'She couldn't wait to tell me that you—you
had been her lover.'

'We had a friendship,' he said grimly, 'and that
hardly rates as a love affair, unless you are so
naïve that you cannot tell the difference—and by
heaven, how naïve you look, *ma chère*, standing
there grasping that towel around you as if a
glimpse of your saintly body is going to turn me
into a ravenous seducer! Why won't you grow up,
eh?'

'Is that what you came to say to me?' Melly
could feel herself shaking with nerves and there

was no way she could keep her inner terrors out of her eyes.

'Not entirely.' He was staring into her eyes as if reading them. 'I realised that Chantal might have said things to upset you, so I came to tell you not to take too much notice of her.'

'Of course.' Melly bit her lip, but she had to go on. 'It's hardly likely that you want me to know of your relationship with her ... of your nude bathing sessions down on the beach. You would want to keep all that from your wife, it's only natural.'

'*Mon Dieu!*' He thrust a hand through his disordered hair. 'You women are all alike, you scratch and claw each other the moment you get together. Aren't you adult enough to realise that after my break with Irene I was in the mood for some crazy behaviour? We did not part without an appalling argument over Jody and because she was going to drag everything into court if I didn't agree to let her have her own way, then for the child's sake I agreed to her terms. What she truly wanted was to come out on top. She wasn't driven by mother love—I was the one who loved Jody!'

He thumped a hand against his chest. 'But how can I expect you to understand? Your innards are all tied up in knots for some reason, so you are bound to think that any fun I had with Chantal was of the lowest kind. I was grateful for her company. She was what I needed at that time— perhaps she still is!'

He swung on his heel and left the room, slamming the door behind him. It clashed so hard into the frame that oddments on the vanity-table made tinkling sounds. Melly flinched as if he had struck her, and it was many minutes before she found the will to dress herself for the evening that lay ahead of her. An evening she must share with two people who shared the memory of that crazy behaviour, as Jourdan had called it. With her gaiety and her inborn knowledge of men Chantal had alleviated Jourdan's distress over Jody, and when a link like that was forged, it wasn't easy to break.

Least of all by a marriage which had turned out to be an unholy mistake.

Tears stung Melly's eyes, but she choked them back. She wouldn't weep and feel sorry for herself. She wouldn't make herself thoroughly abject and miserable, so that by contrast to Chantal she would look pallid and pink-eyed.

'When shall I catch you between wives?' Chantal had asked Jourdan.

Quite soon, it seemed to Melly.

CHAPTER EIGHT

THE back-aching task of clearing the banana groves was finally accomplished and Jourdan employed a couple of men whose task was to keep the pathways raked and clean so that neither weeds nor vermin could flourish again and damage the banana palms. Jourdan's aim was to produce fruit of quality rather than quantity, and he also had to set up a source of shipping and distribution for when the time came to harvest the bananas.

Melly told herself this was the reason why he was absent for hours from the plantation house now the heavy work was behind him and he no longer felt exhausted at the end of the day. She bravely told herself that Jourdan went to town on business, but in her heart she felt certain he was seeing Chantal André.

She tried not to be unhappy about it. He was entitled to find affection in another woman's arms when his marriage to her was such a disappointment. More and more she began to think of leaving him, for they had no lasting future together, and try as she might she was unable to remain indifferent to the thought of him with Chantal.

He and Chantal had so much in common. They were both French and from similar social backgrounds, and though it brought anguish when Melly imagined them in each other's arms, they were so physically suited. When Melly imagined that sleek and silky creature wrapped in

Jourdan's embrace she couldn't quite condemn either of them. It hurt to envisage those red lips clinging to his, the long fingernails unbuttoning his shirt so she could get close to his firm, warm flesh, but it hurt in a sad, resigned way.

Each morning when Melly awoke she told herself that today she would find the courage to pack her bag and walk out of Jourdan's life. She had less of a place in his life than Chantal. She was just a stray girl he had picked up along the way, and she served no purpose except to be an obstacle he would eventually resent.

But her resolution had a way of weakly melting when she sat down to breakfast on the verandah and there was Jourdan looking so big and clean in white shirt and trousers, his black hair brushed smooth by his military brushes, his skin like sun-warmed teak that pulsed beneath with purpose and impulse.

He would smile in that slightly grave way of his and ask if she had slept well, and it was then that jealousy bit her like an asp and she would remember that some of her blood ran in his veins and no matter how many times Chantal kissed him, she could never do for him what Melly had done. The realisation would sweep over her that to live apart from him would be dull and joyless . . . it was hardly to be borne, the thought of never sharing anything with him.

As they drank coffee, crushed as it was from island beans, and ate bacon and eggs, there would drift from the groves the sound of men singing island songs in their deep, rich voices. Tantalising melodies which told of freedom found on the blue water . . . of love in lustrous eyes when the moon sailed the tropic sky.

'How can I go?' Melly would ask herself as she drank Bethula's delicious coffee. 'I'll never be able to forget him . . . never!'

Dramatic as it sounded to herself, she knew that it held the truth. Only the husk of Melly Lanier would return to the lonely life she had lived before meeting Jourdan; her heart and soul would be left behind to haunt the groves of the Lanier plantation. Yet one day soon she had to leave; she couldn't face for very much longer the daily torment of knowing that each polite word from Jourdan might be a concealment for the ardent whispers he left in the ears of Chantal André.

There were mornings when Melly came close to asking him outright if he had been with Chantal the night before. But how could she demand answers to such questions when all she was to him was a wife in name only?

A wife such as herself had fewer rights than a mistress. The vows she had made were as empty as the sea sometimes looked. They were dry bones without any flesh on them. Leaves rustling in a wintry wind, and inevitably they would fall by the wayside as the leaves fell when their season was over.

One morning at breakfast there was a persistent rustling of the palm crests, like leaves of paper in a vagrant wind, and though the sun was shining it was brassy.

Jourdan glanced around at the trees and narrowed his eyes at the sky. 'We could be in for a hurricane,' he said. 'It is the time of the year when one could be brewing, and they come suddenly and strong. Thanks to *le bon Dieu* the groves are in order before a heavy rain sets in.'

'Hurricanes are bad, aren't they?' Melly wasn't

unnerved by the prospect, but she had grown to
care for anything relating to the plantation and
was as proud as Jourdan at how trim and
promising the groves were looking.

'Hurricanes are primitive happenings,' Jourdan
replied, a brief smile twisting his lip. 'Scared by
the possibility?'

She shook her head and peeled a tangerine. 'I
know I look as if the wind might blow me away,
but I'm not a coward.'

'I know you aren't.' His eyes looked deep into
hers and he seemed on the verge of saying
something meaningful ... something that might
relate to his visits to town that extended into the
late hours. Then the look was gone and he asked
for a piece of her fruit.

She broke the tangerine in half and gave him
the section, the juice dripping on to his fingers.
She watched him eat the fruit and deep inside she
was strongly stirred by him ... she wished she
were Chantal André, with the svelte and sensuous
kind of body that appealed to Jourdan. The kind
of woman to whom sensual excitement was as
much love of self as it was of the man she was
involved with.

Jourdan was too worldly not to know all there
was to know about Chantal, and Melly felt
certain that what drew him to the Frenchwoman
was her basic allure. He had loved Irene and
that love had failed, so it was understandable that
he no longer wanted an involvement of the
heart.

'A hurricane can be almighty destructive,' he
said, his dark lashes half lowered across his eyes,
making them thoughtful and unreadable. 'It
becomes necessary to turn the house into a

fortress, with all the shutters securely barred, all the ornaments put away so they won't be broken, then we tuck ourselves away in the cellar and wait for the storm to blow itself out.'

'Would a lot of damage be done to the groves, Jourdan?'

'I fear as much.'

'After all your hard work?' Melly's eyes filled with concern. 'I pray this storm won't be a bad one.'

'It might pass us by, Melly. I think you have grown to like living on the island, have you not?'

She nodded and gazed around the palm court where thickets of hibiscus blended their large flowers with the flaming petals of the orange trumpet vine. The sabred leaves of the tall gum trees fought for supremacy with the shaggy leaves of the palms, and there at the entrance to the groves stood a plumy monarch with violet flowers shaped like huge bells. Each tree and blossom seemed to have a personality of its own, just like the exotic birds that flew among the scented petals and leaves. One bird was a delight, being a cross between a bee-eater and a kingfisher, with a bronze-green body and a long pendulous tail who called 'coo-coo' as it flew into the green cathedral of the banana groves.

Melly could no more resist the spell of the island than she could resist the temptation to marry Jourdan, knowing in her heart that a marriage such as theirs was doomed to failure.

'How much I shall miss all this——' Melly broke off in mid-sentence, a catch of relief in her throat when she noticed that Jourdan had become engrossed in a letter he had just opened.

'This is from Jody,' he said in a quiet, too

controlled voice. 'She informs me that she likes her new "papa", that he has a yacht and the three of them go sailing at the weekends. She spends five days at her school, but Roy, as she refers to him, insists that she spend Saturday and Sunday with him and her mother. It seems he cuts a very romantic figure in his yachting outfit and he and Jody have become fantastic friends. I am told that he's a very different "papa" from myself, always away as I was, guarding Arab princes and such personages.'

He paused, and there was anger in his sigh. 'It would seem, Melly, that my child's vocabulary has improved, but her fondness for me has ebbed away on this tide of admiration for her mother's new husband.'

Melly watched, not knowing what to say as Jourdan refolded the letter and tucked it away in the envelope, which he tossed down on the table. When he met Melly's eyes she saw the pain etched into his face, darkening his eyes to slate-grey . . . storm-shaded grey.

'So now I know,' he said grimly, 'this man Roy is now the hero in my daughter's life!'

'Don't—don't mind too much, Jourdan.' Melly hesitated, then slid a hand towards his and touched it, feeling his fingers clench beneath hers. 'After all, Jody is only a child and she doesn't realise that her words might have a point to them. Children just speak from the heart——'

'Yes, from the heart,' he agreed curtly, 'and that is what hurts.'

'Of course it does—it's bound to.'

'From now onwards Jody and I will become strangers.'

'You mustn't believe that, Jourdan.'

'I have to face it. Irene's new husband is obviously good to Jody and I thank him for that, but it means that inevitably I am going to lose her to him.' Jourdan stood up and stared rather blindly across the palm court. Melly gazed up at him and wished she could take that look of loss out of his eyes. That was the trouble with a broken marriage, hearts got broken as well and sometimes there was no mending them.

'I have to go into town,' he said abruptly. 'I have a business appointment connected with the groves—would you like to come along, Melly?'

The abrupt invitation took her by surprise. 'Do you mean it, Jourdan?'

He glanced at her, frowning impatiently. 'Why should I not mean it?'

'I—I don't want to be in your way.' Somehow after that letter from Jody he could be in need of some comforting, and it wouldn't have surprised Melly had he wanted to go and see Chantal. It wasn't that the child had been cruel on purpose, for she was only stating her point of view, but he had looked like a man who had been kicked. Jody wouldn't understand until she grew up that her father had worked for his country and risked his neck in ways that took a great deal of courage and stamina.

'You won't be in the way.' His eyes flicked over her as if he was thinking that Melly looked very young and hardly took up much room, least of all in his thoughts.

'Then I'd like to come very much.' Melly pushed back her chair and stood up; she was wearing shorts and a shirt, as she had intended to spend the morning down on the beach. 'It won't take me long to change—you'll wait for me?'

'Of course I shall wait.' As she went to hurry away he caught her by the wrist and detained her. 'You are an odd sort of girl, aren't you, *mon enfant*? You have, I believe, a fixation about being intrusive—*mon Dieu*, you are the least intrusive person I have ever known!'

His eyes looking directly down at her confused her and she felt her skin flushing. He was no doubt comparing her to Chantal, who had such self-assured vivacity. It would never even occur to Chantal to think she might not be welcome anywhere.

'I have neglected you these past few weeks.' Jourdan held her gaze as firmly as he held her wrist. 'But it was necessary that I put the groves in order, and there have been contacts to make with regard to making the groves a viable business venture. You do understand?'

'Absolutely,' she assured him, almost holding her breath as he carried her hand to his lips and kissed the inside of her wrist. She felt the warm pressure of his mouth against her skin, then he freed her so she could go and change into a dress.

But from small acorns grow the oaks and Melly wished she could entirely believe him when he implied that his absences were connected with the banana business. Only the other morning Bethula had found a lace-edged handkerchief on the floor of Jourdan's bedroom and thinking it belonged to Melly she had brought it to her. There had been a smear of deep red lipstick on the fabric and Melly could only assume that it had fallen from Jourdan's pocket ... a handkerchief which Chantal had probably handed to him so he could wipe his mouth after they had kissed goodnight. Absently he had put the handkerchief into his pocket and brought it home with him, a telltale sign of his involvement with Chantal.

Be that as it may, Melly was eager to be with him even if, like the day itself, there were ominous signs of a storm that might break and engulf them at any time. After all, it was to her that Jourdan had turned in his unhappiness over Jody's unthinking letter. Chantal André represented excitement rather than a deeper understanding of his dilemma where Jody was concerned.

Chantal was worldly, but she wasn't wise in Melly's way. Melly knew how to be compassionate even if she shrank from physical passion. Right now she felt wanted as a friend and that was sufficient, and she zipped herself into a summery dress with a scooped neck, dashed pink lipstick over her mouth and returned to Jourdan with a look of bright expectancy in her eyes.

He waited beside the bonnet of the car and he watched her through the smoke of a cheroot as she approached him. Her colour mounted again as his grey eyes slid up and down her figure in the shantung dress of honey-gold.

'The colour matches your eyes,' he remarked.

'Th-thank you.' She glanced at the sky. 'Do you think I should take an umbrella with me?'

'Melly,' he broke into a laugh, 'you are matchless! An umbrella would soon turn itself inside out if a blow overtakes the island.' He tossed away the remainder of his cheroot and opened the door of the car. He stood there as she slid into her seat and she knew from the tensing of his nostrils that he had caught a whiff of the scent she had applied a little too generously from an atomiser which had a tendency to stick and then spurt.

'Very nice,' he murmured. 'Are you trying to entice me?'

'No, as if I would!' Her heart palpitated and she nervously smoothed the skirt of her dress, hearing the whisper of the soft fabric beneath the touch of her fingers. When Jourdan slid behind the wheel his long leg brushed against hers and she became intensely aware of his big frame beside her, in the enclosed intimacy of the car. The feeling made her feel breathless ... shy ... frightened.

Carefully she moved her leg away from his, but he seemed not to notice her withdrawal from contact with him. He was driving out of the gateway when a palm leaf whipped down against the windscreen and was splayed there a moment like a large hand, then it blew to the ground.

'The wind has more force in it,' he murmured. 'Are you certain you want to come with me, Melly? We could be stranded in town if a big blow hits the island.'

'I—I'd sooner be with you, Jourdan, than alone at the house.' The thought of them being separated during the roar and fury of a possible hurricane sent shivers through Melly.

'You would not be alone,' he said. 'You would have the company of Bethula and the workers.'

'Oh, very well,' Melly caught hold of the door handle, 'if you don't really want me with you——'

'If you'd sooner go on your own——'

'Don't be childish!'

'Y-you're always saying I'm childish——' She felt a threatening sting of tears, for it seemed to her that he really wanted to be with Chantal ...

the onset of a hurricane would be a plausible excuse for him to be stranded in town.

'Sometimes you act like a child.' He spoke curtly as he drove beneath the arching trees that shaded them until they reached the highway. Melly sank back against the leather of her seat and realised that the edginess between them was growing more intense, as if both of them were living on their nerves and would inevitably find it impossible to go on living in the same house.

'Are you seeing someone important?' she asked him eventually.

'Important to the groves; he's a shipper and a reputable one and I want to come to terms with him. You would find it tiresome to sit in on our discussion, so I shall let you off in town and you can have a wander around the market place. You will find it colourful and appealing—have you any money so you can buy yourself a handbag or a trinket . . . even a monkey if you should feel like it?'

She smiled a little and relaxed. 'I don't spend half the money you give me for the housekeeping, so I've plenty to spend.'

'How easily satisfied you are, *mignonne*!' He cast a quick look at her, as if yet again she had managed to make him curious, and just a little bit impatient. 'Most women want all they can get from a man.'

'Oh, what a very cynical remark, Jourdan!' She met his eyes for the brief moment he took his attention from the road. 'You confuse us all with—with Irene.'

'Perhaps I do,' he admitted. 'I can just imagine her face if I suggested that she wander around the market place and buy herself a trinket. How amazingly different the two of you are!'

'It worries you that we are, doesn't it, Jourdan?' Melly spoke quietly, unable to help it that he found her mysterious and so elusive compared to someone like Chantal. Yet she was quite certain that Chantal was cut from the same velvet and venom as Irene.

'I have to admit that I don't fully understand you, Melly. As I may have said once before, you have a simplicity which conceals complexity, and though most women are difficult to fathom, you are beyond doubt a mystery I can't seem to solve.'

'It's best not to try,' Melly murmured.

'It worries you that I might try, eh?'

She chose not to answer him; adroitly as possible she changed the trend of the conversation. 'Bethula saves us a lot of money by buying our groceries from the local farmers, and she's so honest and scrupulous. It's so good to eat big brown eggs that actually boil without breaking. Back home I used to hate eating eggs because I knew they'd been laid by poor battery hens. Bethula says the hens at Jake's farm run loose all over the place, and so do the pigs.'

'Do you realise what you are experiencing, Melly?' A note of indulgence warmed Jourdan's voice. 'It's a sense of freedom, of being among people who are brown and warm as those eggs. Life here on Bel-Aze would have been the making of Jody, but I have to forget it—I have to let it go. Will you help me to do that?'

'If I can, Jourdan.' She slanted a look at his profile and saw how firm and determined it was.

'Is that a promise?'

'Yes.'

'I shall expect you to keep that promise.'

'I—I know you will.'

'I'm not speaking lightly, Melly. My aim is to make the plantation one of the best, and everything I do from now on will be in the utmost interest of the groves. I want them to flourish ... I want to put down roots in the soil of the island. It has become of foremost importance to me, you realise that?'

'Of course I do, Jourdan.' All Melly could give him was enthusiasm for his plans, but in her honesty she couldn't share them in the way of a real wife. The very way he talked about putting down roots made her aware that she must pull hers free before her heartstrings became so entangled around Jourdan that it would wrench her apart to leave him. Her only usefulness had lain in being a companion to his child, who only today had written him a letter in which she referred to another man as her papa.

It had deeply hurt Jourdan, but at the same time it had intensified his wish to make a real and lasting life on the island.

'I do like the sound of your plans,' Melly said softly.

'You believe they stand a chance of coming true?' he asked.

'Oh yes! You'll make things happen your way because you're strong and certain and you don't recognise defeat. In view of the way things turned out regarding Jody, you would have been justified had you thrown in your hand and left the banana groves to rot. Instead you set to and brought order where chaos ruled. Yes, Jourdan, you are one of the strong people who doesn't break.'

'You flatter me, Melly, but I like it.'

She smiled, but inside herself she was already releasing him, letting go of a man she couldn't hope to hold. That vibrant strength of his was not meant to be wasted on a sterile marriage, and already Melly was sure that she had lost part of him to Chantal André . . . willing and eager in his arms, offering him more than words of encouragement.

'Yes,' he said forcefully, 'I shall make things happen my way! The future lies ahead, and what is in the past is like a snapshot which gradually loses its clarity. The image dims, the picture fades, and new aspects take predominance.'

Some time later they drove into the colourful township of Bel-Aze, where market stalls and cafés lined the quayside. Solid cobbled walls guarded the town and the remains of an old fortress stood with its sea-greened cannons. Below the walls the sea reflected the brassy glow of the sun, and the market place teemed with shoppers despite the rising wind that whipped the palm crests and slurped the waves up against the sea wall.

Jourdan let Melly out of the car and directed her attention to a nearby plaza where there was a rococo bandstand and café tables beneath gaily striped awnings. 'You see that café by the fountain, Melly? I shall meet you there in about an hour and in the meantime have a saunter around the shops and stalls—and don't lose yourself!'

He smiled as he scanned her face, the sun glinting in his eyes. On impulse Melly leaned down into the car and kissed his cheek, then she drew away from him, stepping back across the barrier she had erected between them.

'How did I manage to earn a kiss?' He looked
quizzically up at her, his face dark and definite
and just a little mystified.

She felt the silent thunder of her heart as she
gazed back at him ... how very much she loved
him, and yet it was a statement she could never
make.

'Oh, I'm trying in my awkward way to make
up for that letter,' she rejoined. 'I could see how
hurt you felt—you did say, didn't you, that I
should behave like a daughter to you?'

'Did I say that?' He looked her up and down in
the honey-gold dress that the wind pressed
against her figure. 'I had quite forgotten that I
ever said such a nonsensical thing to you! Take
care, *mignonne!*'

He drove off along the narrow road that snaked
its way through the town where the traffic
jangled as shoppers stepped in and out of the
road with a casual disregard for safety. Some of
the women carried their shopping baskets on the
crown of the head, their deportment as easy and
graceful as that of highly-paid models.

Melly stood bemused by the scene, so alive
with colour and spiciness and the sound of the
bargain-hunters as they jostled around the stalls,
carefree and friendly. Tropic fruits were heaped
high; the kind of fruits which Bethula turned into
delicious desserts. Cantaloupe melons, crimson
mango, the litchi with its apple-like skin, the
deep-green plantain, and guavas that filled the air
with their sweetness.

All sorts of goods were on display, and Melly
paused to admire a silver-bronze slave bracelet,
unaware that her sunlit hair was attracting
attention. Should she buy the bracelet? It would

make a charming keepsake to take back to England, yet always it would remind her that she had been enslaved by a man.

In broken English the stallholder urged her to buy the trinket, but Melly shook her head and replaced it among the other items that gleamed and glittered like fool's gold.

Instead she bought herself a nectarine and wandered along eating it. She turned into a cobbled alleyway and climbed a twisting flight of street steps to where a break in the wall showed glimpses of the wind-ruffled sea. The sound of calypso music drifted from an open window and drew her towards some raffish little shops, dens of discovery where she paused to admire a machete in a studded sheath.

Quite suddenly, and quite badly, she wanted to buy it for Jourdan, and she went inside the shop to ask the price.

The woman who sat behind the counter shelling peas into a wooden bowl had a gleaming dark face beneath a bright bandana, her eyes like onyx as she scanned Melly, taking in the delicacy of her appearance. Then she arose, took the machete out of the window and slowly drew the African weapon from the sheath.

'This for a big lion of a man,' she said, with a flash of her strong white teeth.

'That's why I want it,' said Melly. 'How much are you asking for it?'

A price was suggested, and Melly remembered what Bethula had told her, that she must always bargain with the island traders. They expected it and respected a good bargainer.

'That's a bit too much,' she said firmly. 'That ornamentation on the sheath is copper, not gold.'

'You are uppity *anglaise*, eh?' But still the woman smiled, as if she liked a show of spirit. 'Men die to dig out copper just as they perish to dig out gold.'

'That might well be the case,' Melly rejoined, 'but you know full well you're asking too much for the knife.'

'This blade very sharp, *petite*, chop off your head.'

'I daresay.' If the woman had hoped to make Melly shudder she didn't succeed. 'If you want the earth for it, then I'll look round for something else.'

As Melly started to walk out of the shop the trader called her back. The bargain was sealed and the machete was wrapped, then as Melly paid over the money her hand was suddenly caught and held in the strong dark fingers. She met the woman's eyes, abruptly aware that she had wandered into the sideways, a foreign girl entirely on her own. She was tensing her fingers when her hand was turned over so her palm could be scanned; at once she relaxed, for Bethula had told her about the *obeah* men and women who were supposed to have occult powers.

'You are troubled,' the woman said slowly, 'and in your hand, *petite*, I see a crossroads.'

'Oh, we all have troubles,' Melly said lightly. 'I've had my share, of course.'

'This dark, haunting kind I don't see often in a young hand.' The onyx eyes looked deeply into Melly's. 'Be very careful which road you take ... one leads to nowhere.'

'Oh——' Melly's hand went tense again in the woman's grip, 'I won't be frightened by what you say! Please let go of me, I have to meet my husband for lunch.'

'For him you buy the machete, eh?'

'Yes.'

'Don't cut out your heart with it.' The woman released Melly's hand and resuming her seat, she started to shell peas again. Melly said a hurried goodbye, those last words going round and round in her mind as she hastened down the weathered steps that led to the quayside. Palm reading was a lot of nonsense, she told herself. These islands in the tropics abounded with superstition, and the stormy expectancy of the day added a kind of strangeness to mood and scene.

Clutching her parcel, she made her way to where Jourdan had suggested they meet for lunch, and she was aware as she sat down that her legs were trembling. She was being idiotic, allowing a stranger in a shop to upset her nerves with some foolish talk about a crossroads that led to nowhere. Yet the words held a significance which Melly couldn't completely ignore. Her life with Jourdan had reached a kind of fork, and if she took the path that led her back to England she would be leaving her heart behind her and it would feel as if it had been cut from her body.

She gave a painful gasp and pressed a hand to her left side, feeling there an emptiness that was tangible as the brassy warmth of the sun, real as the petals that drifted down from a golden shower-tree, shaken loose by the wind in its branches. They brushed Melly with their softness, like fragrant confetti such as people tossed upon a bride in her satin and lace, clinging to the arm of a man who loved her madly . . . beyond face and form.

Somewhere below the quayside a man was singing, his voice deep and rich, and as Melly listened she made out the words. *Sail away . . . sail away and don't you grieve. There are girls you love. There are girls you leave. Sail away . . . sail away.*

'Melly?'

She glanced up, startled out of her thoughts, her wide eyes collecting into them the tall figure in the cool white suit.

'There you are!' She stood up too quickly and stumbled, into the swift arms that held her strongly . . . her head spun, her heart throbbed, her every nerve thrilled to his touch.

'You have a touch of the sun, eh?' His eyes dwelt on her hair and roamed her face. 'What have you bought yourself?'

'I bought a present for you, Jourdan. I hope you'll like it.'

'You should not spend your pocket money on me,' he protested. 'Being a daughter to me again, is that it?'

She nodded, for it was a safe little bolthole, this pretence that she felt like a daughter to him. 'I lost my own father when I was an infant, so it's nice to—to pretend.'

'Pretend, *mon enfant*, if it makes you happy.'

They found a shady table and when they were seated Melly handed Jourdan his present. She noticed that he opened it like a man who wasn't used to receiving gifts, and as she watched him she felt as if a hand clutched her by the throat, suppressing all that she dared not say to him. How much he wrenched at her heart, shades of the boy showing in the firm-shouldered man when he glanced up from admiring the machete, his eyes reflecting the steely blade. 'This is a real beauty,' he said warmly. 'The scrolling on the sheath is genuine artwork—how did you come to find it?'

'In a funny little shop up one of the side streets.' She felt a ripple of pleasure at the pleased look in his eyes. 'I thought it would look good on the wall of your den.'

'You unexpected child!' He leaned forward, his eyes holding hers. 'I thank you very much indeed for thinking of me.'

Melly rarely stopped thinking of him, but it was something she couldn't tell him. 'Just a keepsake,' she said airily. 'Did your business talk go well?'

'Melly, I have clinched a very good deal, so I think we shall celebrate with a bottle of pink champagne. Do you remember the last time we had it?'

'At the Ritz.' She glanced around her and felt keenly how the ambience of Bel-Aze had crept under her skin. 'It was nice to dine there, Jourdan, but I like this place so much more. The island people have no falseness; they're so real and caring. They are *themselves*.'

Jourdan gave her a very intent look and her heart seemed to miss a beat. Was he thinking that she concealed her real self? Was he wondering what her secret was? Did he suspect as they sat here in the sun that this might be the last time they would drink champagne together?

'Bel-Aze has crept into your blood, Melly, just as it crept into mine the first time I came here. Right away I wanted to have a house on this island; a retreat to which I could come when the so-called civilised world got on my nerves. The world beyond its shores is well lost so far as I am concerned—do you feel that way?'

She nodded and thrust away from her the necessity she felt to leave Jourdan and the island. Bel-Aze had cast a spell over her, but the islander who had sold her the machete had seen the threat of a parting.

Melly lifted her gaze to the sky, where the sun brooded in a globe of brass, and from all directions there was a persistent rustling of the palm trees, whose very tallness seemed to catch the threat of a coming storm that would lash at them with its rain-whips and its lightning.

That molten glow of the sun, Melly noticed, seemed to intensify the tangy aroma of spices and fruit and warm-skinned people. She felt herself breathing it all in as Jourdan asked their waiter to chill their champagne. In the meantime they had long glasses of passionfruit juice while they awaited their first course of fresh-hauled lobster.

'Mmmm, this is delicious.' Melly drank her juice thirstily.

'Did no one ever tell you that passion can also be that way?' Jourdan smiled with the edge of his mouth, but his eyes stayed intent upon her face as if he meant to catch her reaction to his remark.

She didn't evade his eyes; to do so might have told him more than she wished him to know. 'I'll have to get Bethula to show me how to make this drink,' she said innocently.

Jourdan's eyes narrowed to slits of steel, then with a slight shake of his head he leaned back in his chair. Their lobster arrived at the table, served with a smooth sauce and a stack of bread and butter. Melly tucked in hungrily, and never had she tasted shellfish so sweet and meaty. She

and Gran had never had money enough to afford
lobster, and her thoughts took flight and landed
her in a cottage garden where she had stood the
day of her grandmother's burial and bade
goodbye to all she had loved and known since a
small child. Her sense of loss had been so acute
that she had been unable to cry. It was as if the
tears had crystallised inside her, hurting like
shards of glass, refusing to melt so she could find
relief from her loneliness . . . from her initial fear
of facing the world all alone.

'You have gone far away, *mignonne*.' Jourdan's
voice broke in on her thoughts. 'Don't go
wandering down memory lane, Melly, where the
shadows are. I know when you are doing so
because the shadows creep into your eyes.'

'I—I was thinking about my grandmother. She
had so few holidays in her life . . . she worked so
hard, and the rewards were few.'

'I'm aware that life picks and chooses its
favourites, *mon enfant*, and that very often the
nicest people receive the hardest deal, but all we
can do is get on with the business of living and
make the most of the hand we are dealt. You
must come to terms with it, once and for all.'

She nodded, and it was then that the first
rumble of thunder came in over the sea, a drawn-
out boom like air trapped in a giant seashell.

'The storm!' she exclaimed.

'Yes,' he inclined his head, 'the blow is on its
way, but we have time in which to enjoy our
lunch.'

The lobster was followed by lamb, crisp baked
with buttered courgettes, glazed carrots and
parsnips. Their chilled champagne was served,
and Jourdan said quizzically:

'I think it might be a good idea if we stay in town.' He studied the glass of champagne in his hand and he looked casual enough. 'We can book into the Beaumont, a hotel above the bay.'

'But, Jourdan,' Melly felt a stab of panic as she gazed across the table at him, 'w-what about nightwear and toothbrushes?'

'My dear child, we can buy those.' He looked up at the sky which had begun to lower itself upon the island rather like a brass lid that was shutting in the heat. Traders had begun to clear and close their stalls and a sense of urgency had replaced the carefree atmosphere and silenced the laughter.

Melly felt her skin tighten; she shivered in the heat.

'I—I think we should make for home,' she said, almost a note of pleading in her voice.

'What are you afraid of, Melly?' Slowly he tipped champagne into his mouth and watched her as he swallowed. 'Is it the storm you fear, or is it me?'

'No,' she protested, knowing in her heart that he represented far more danger to her than the storm ever could. 'I know it isn't wise to drink and drive, but w-we could take a cab home. You could leave the car parked in town.'

'We could do both those things,' he agreed rather mockingly, 'but we aren't going to. The hotel is a very interesting one and it will only take us a few minutes to drive up. It will make a break for both of us, and we shall be able to watch the antics of the storm from the glassed-in terrace. Usually there is a dance on Saturday nights— remember how we danced together on the ship?'

'I—I'm not exactly dressed for dancing.' She tried to speak lightly, but her heart was thumping; half of her wanted so much to stay.

but the other half knew that it would only lead to disaster. 'Jourdan, let's go home!'

'No, Melly.' His jaw was set and it was obvious to her that he had made up his mind that they were going to have a weekend in town.

'Bethula will be worried about us.' It was a last-ditch attempt to persuade him to change his mind.

He shook his head and there was a gleam of amusement in his eyes. 'I told her we would stay in town if the hurricane came this way.'

'So—so you had it all planned?' Melly's fingers tightly gripped the stem of her champagne glass.

'Let us say I had it half planned.' He moved his gaze over her apprehensive face. 'What is worrying you, *ma chère*? The bedroom accommodation?'

She flushed. 'Y-you know how I feel——'

'Do I, Melly?'

She gazed back at him uncertainly. 'You aren't going to insist that I—I——?'

'Can't you put it into words, Melly?'

'You're being cruel, Jourdan!' She felt a flash of temper. 'You know my feelings on that subject.'

'Then will it satisfy you if I say that I shall book us into separate rooms?'

She nodded and lowered her gaze, unable to bear it that he should think her such a prude. She drank the champagne in her glass hoping it would steady her nerves, which seemed to be fluttering like live things in her pelvis.

They continued with their lunch, and Melly was fully aware of the irony in Jourdan's eyes as they ate passionfruit chiffon pie for dessert.

In a while as they made their way to the shops she heard a seabird calling in the storm mottled sky. 'If only . . . if only . . .' it seemed to cry.

CHAPTER NINE

THE Beaumont on the Hill was one of those mid-Victorian hotels which time had left stranded on its own bluff overlooking the bay of Bel-Aze.

The building had immense windows, castellated rooftops and large balconies enclosed in ornamental iron. The lift was in an iron cage which rattled ponderously as it carried Melly and Jourdan to the floor where their rooms were situated.

The porter led them along a quiet corridor and opened the door of what turned out to be adjoining bedrooms and bathroom *en suite*, the carpets of faded Turkish design, the furniture in bold mahogany, the high ceilings equipped with large fans that circulated the humid air. After laying her parcels down on the bed of her own room Melly went across to the big window and gazed out upon a balcony that extended to a parapet. The rain had started and there were intermittent flashes of lightning, and although it was only four o'clock in the afternoon a premature dusk had fallen upon the island, punctured by lights down in the bay.

The gusts of wind rattled the windows, strong enough to rock the car as they had driven uphill to the hotel. Melly had heard a booming sound and Jourdan told her it was the storm guns being fired, warning the islanders that a tempestuous blow was building up and they had better prepare for it by hurrying home and fastening their doors and shutters.

Melly was still watching the rain when Jourdan came and joined her at the window, silent for a while as the wind whined at the glass and tossed the foliage of the balcony plants back and forth.

'Looks as if the end of the world is coming,' he commented. 'Fortunately we are under cover, though it isn't going to be a force twelve according to the porter. He told me he has been listening to the radio reports which are relayed from ships in the vicinity. Tracking planes will have flown to the disturbed area in order to locate the eye of the storm and assess the direction in which it will move. Like most things connected with the elements the unpredictable can happen.'

'Is a force twelve a really bad one?' As Melly looked out upon the dramatic masses of cloud, silvered at the edges, she felt it had been the right thing to do, to come to the hotel instead of trying to drive home in the gale-driven rain.

'Even a lesser hurricane can do a hell of a lot of damage,' Jourdan replied. 'I would predict that this one is going to be showy, and we are in the right atmosphere to watch it. I rather like these hotels to which clings an air of colonial living . . . even of romantic rendezvous, when women took the time to be charming; when it hadn't entered their heads to compete with men.'

'Times change,' Melly remarked, though she felt just as responsive to the ambience of the Beaumont; had felt it directly they entered the vestibule with its tall marble columns.

'But not always for the better.' Jourdan shot a look at his wristwatch. 'Do you fancy some tea? They serve it down in one of the lounge rooms; cucumber sandwiches and freshly baked cakes.'

'Mmm, yes, I would like that.' Melly turned to

him with a smile which changed to a flinch as a
loud clap of thunder shook the windows.

'Don't tell me a country-bred girl is afraid of
thunder,' he mocked. 'A girl who rode moorland
ponies——' There he broke off, for a lurid flash
of lightning showed him the whiteness of Melly's
face. 'You are afraid, eh?'

'N-no——' She shook her head. 'It isn't so
much fear as excitement; it sort of winds me up.'

Jourdan gripped her by the elbow and studied
her face, all eyes and translucent skin, her hair a
mane of lightness as she stood there looking up at
him. The moment stretched, filled with storm
sounds that seemed to recede to the very edge of
Melly's awareness as Jourdan searched her eyes,
looking down deep as if curious about the girl
who had ridden across the moors, her hair flying
in the wind, her heart young and light and
unafraid.

'What is thunder,' he drawled, 'but two
heavenly bodies forced into contact by electricity
in the atmosphere? As if, Melly, you would be
afraid of such a happening! Come, let us go in
search of tea and sandwiches!'

They walked down the grand staircase which
showed its age but was still a gracious tribute to
the days when a dance dress swept the carpet
with its flounces and was shown off against the
wrought-iron of the balustrade.

Tea was served in the Empire lounge by
waitresses in the traditional cap and apron, and
there was a pianist at the grand piano playing
melodies from another time, nostalgic and
tuneful. It was as if the guests who came through
the doors of the Beaumont were eager for the
clock to be turned back so they could forget for a

while the problems of coping with present-day life.

Melly shared a sofa with Jourdan and poured their tea from a swan-necked pot into china cups with golden rims. There was cube sugar in a bowl and a little pair of tongs to lift the sugar. The cakes were invitingly arranged on a stand, and the cucumber sandwiches were cut into triangles.

Jourdan lounged back comfortably with his cup of tea and looked around him with an air of quiet pleasure. Gone was his mood of the morning, and as Melly watched him there was no way she could keep herself from wondering if he ever brought Chantal André to the Beaumont. Had they ever danced here together ... loved here together?

She tried to thrust away such hurtful thoughts, but there seemed no way to forget that he had said Chantal was fun to be with. Though Melly told herself she had no right to feel possessive of him, she just couldn't help it when she looked at him. Right now he looked at peace with himself, as if no one beyond the doors of the hotel infringed upon his present state of well-being.

His eyes met hers and he smiled lazily. 'Clever of the management to have made time stand still. This is something we all need to experience when life becomes a problem.'

Melly wondered if he considered her a problem. Did it sometimes occur to him that if she walked out on their marriage he would then be free to be with Chantal as often as he desired?

'More tea, Jourdan?' She spoke composedly but didn't feel totally at ease. Her troubled thoughts combined with the storm in the air to make her jumpy.

'If you please.' He handed his cup to her and reached for a cake. 'You like to dance, don't you, Melly? I thought on the ship that you were quite a young Ginger Rogers, though I cannot say of myself that I am a Fred Astaire.' His lip quirked. 'Tell me, you must have had a boy-friend or two. Come, confess!'

'W-we had dances at the village hall—hops, as we called them.' Carefully she poured the tea, intent on controlling her nerves, and it was something of a relief when the cup and saucer was back in his hand.

'There was no local young man on whom you had a crush?' Alone with her like this he seemed to want to quench his curiosity as well as his thirst, and his eyes didn't leave her face as he drank his tea.

'I liked being with Gran—and the horses.' She managed a slight smile. 'I've never been the flirtatious sort. Perhaps I was born with a serious nature.'

'Perhaps so.' He bit into his cake. 'There are quite a few things I don't know about you, and you don't intend to enlighten me, do you?'

'All of us are entitled to have a little cabinet in the mind where we keep things under lock and key,' she replied.

'That is true, but some of the things we lock away, *mignonne*, can sometimes do more harm than good. You say you enjoyed being with the horses, yet why did you leave the riding school? It wasn't entirely to do with your grandmother dying, was it?'

'It was,' she said, obstinately.

'You left beautiful Devon, work you thrived on, just to go and be a hospital maid in London. Won't you tell me the true reason?'

'Y-you're being very persistent, Jourdan.' She shifted nervously. 'Too much reminded me of Gran—I had to make a life elsewhere!'

'But why seek that new life in a hospital, Melly?'

'I enjoyed it. It was satisfying to see people get better—remember how you asked me for a big juicy steak? That was a sure sign that you were recovering.'

His eyes strayed over her face. 'Have you ever been ill yourself?'

Her heart gave an alarming throb there behind her breastbone. 'I—I had the usual childhood complaints.'

'No doubt.' He studied her thoughtfully. 'I have sometimes wondered if it was an operation that gave the clinic their knowledge of the blood group you share with me.'

'They knew because I—I had to have iron pills.'

He tapped a cheroot against his case and still he had an interrogative glint in his eyes. 'Did the pills help you?'

'Yes. I'm perfectly all right now.'

'What caused you to be delicate in the first place?'

'Not eating my greens like a good child,' she rejoined. 'Really, Jourdan, when you start to ask questions it's like being with Sherlock Holmes!'

'Are you enjoying those stories of his exploits? I saw the volume on your bedside table the other night.'

'The other night?' she echoed, feeling again as if her heart bounced against her bones.

'You were having a bad dream, I think. You cried out and I came into your room to ask what was wrong but you were sound asleep. You had half thrown off your covers, so I tucked you in again and then returned to my own room. Perhaps you had read a mysterious story which played on your mind, eh?'

She glanced down at her hands, which had folded tightly together in her lap. 'I hope I didn't wake you from a sound sleep, Jourdan.'

He shook his head. 'I had not long arrived home.'

'I see.' She looked away from him, surmising that he had been with Chantal. She tensed in every fibre when Jourdan laid a hand on her shoulder, his fingers striking warm through the soft fabric of her dress.

'Do you mind if I happen to see you in your sleep?' he asked, a shading of irony in his voice. 'For the love of heaven! Do you think I was going to jump in beside you—you looked as young and innocent as a child, your hair tousled and the covers disarranged around you! I don't practise assault on helpless girls!'

Melly jerked away from him, a reflex action caused by his words rather than his touch. 'You would hardly be in that sort of mood, anyway,' she said defensively.

'I don't catch your meaning,' his eyes narrowed, 'though it would seem that I am meant to.'

'You don't have to pretend with me, Jourdan.' Melly took a steadying breath. 'I realise that you've been seeing Chantal André, and I don't blame you. I—I know I'm the one in the wrong! You should go for an annulment and have a proper marriage——'

'Be quiet!'

'W-what?' She gazed at him startled.

'You heard me.'

Silently she gazed at him while from across the lounge stole the sound of piano music, a nocturne of rather melancholy beauty that suited the mood of the day; of a hotel isolated from the town, across whose ceiling-high windows the full curtains had been pulled in order to shut out the lightning and muffle the sound of thunder. If the storm increased in velocity the great shutters would be closed, but for the time being the rain and wind were not at full pitch.

Melly heard the music distantly and felt as if the thunder was inside her.

'Listen to me,' Jourdan leaned towards her and dominated her with his gaze, 'if I wanted an annulment of our marriage I would propose one, and that would be final. Furthermore, if I wanted another battle of the sexes I would certainly choose Chantal to give it to me. But as it happens I have no further taste for hemlock!'

'Hemlock?' Melly gasped.

'Poison, *ma chère*. Looking like wine and tasting like hell!'

'I—I don't understand you, Jourdan.' She gave him a bewildered look; she had so managed to convince herself that he was having an affair with Chantal that it seemed unbelievable to hear him talking in this way.

'I had no idea I was talking Swahili.' He looked exasperated. 'Do you really believe that I have been seeing Chantal behind your back? You surely must know that I have been having discussions regarding the running of the groves.'

'Bethula found a lace handkerchief on the floor of your room.' The words burst from Melly. 'She thought it belonged to me—there was a lipstick mark on it.'

He frowned, then abruptly a light dawned in his eyes. 'You must realise, Melly, that the tropical suits I have been wearing have been kept at the plantation house ever since my parting from Irene. Quite obviously one of her handkerchiefs was in one of my pockets.'

'Oh—yes.' As Melly's mouth made a soft sound of realisation Jourdan leaned closer and laid a smoky kiss against her lips.

'Does that kiss it better?' he murmured.

A flush showed through her skin and ran into the roots of her hair. 'I—I'm sorry, Jourdan, for being so suspicious.'

'No doubt I would be suspicious of you, child, if I found a great square of cambric fallen from your pocket.' He smiled, then gestured at a solitary mooncake left on the cake stand. 'Do eat that cake, it looks so lonely.'

She picked up the cake and bit into nuts and fruit, then as she leaned back against the cushions of the sofa, a tremendous clap of thunder shook the hotel, and moments later members of the staff began to secure the window shutters.

Jourdan gave a brief laugh as the pianist began to play *Stormy Weather*.

Before starting their drive up to the Beaumont they had gone shopping for toiletries and nightwear. Jourdan had insisted on buying Melly a long-skirted dress of peachy chiffon, declaring that she had to have a proper dance dress in keeping with the ambience of the hotel. His white suit would pass muster so long as he purchased a dress shirt and a black tie.

So here they were, going down to dine and looking, according to Jourdan, like a couple out of *The Tatler*. As they were shown to a table in the large, rococo dining-room, Melly noticed that most of the women were clad in ordinary dresses.

'You could have saved yourself some money,' she told Jourdan. 'People are looking at the pair of us as if they think we're on our—honeymoon.'

His eyes glimmered in the light of the rose-shaded table lamp. 'Then let us pretend that they are right, eh?'

Her throat went dry and she strove not to look as apprehensive as she suddenly felt. She reached for water and her hand shook as she poured some into her glass.

'Have you come over faint?' Jourdan looked mocking, and when the wine waiter came to the table he deliberately ordered a bottle of Perrier Jouet, whose progress to the table in an ice-bucket was avidly watched by diners nearby.

'Are the gardenias your idea as well?' Melly touched them in their vase as she spoke, wondering what she was going to do about this man she kept trying not to love.

In a way she had wanted to believe that he was having an affair with Chantal; it would have given her a valid reason to leave him. But his denial left her in no doubt that he was telling the truth. For a while Chantal had attracted him because she had something of Irene in her look and manner . . . and she had disenchanted him for all the same reasons which had led to the breakdown of his marriage. Inevitably he had realised that Chantal loved only herself and had no room in her heart for anyone else. She wasn't the type to care what a man was like beneath his skin; all that really mattered to her was that being seen with an attractive man proved that she was attractive.

'Don't you care for gardenias?'

Melly gave a little start as Jourdan's voice broke in on her thoughts. 'They're very pretty,' she replied.

'They are like you, *mignonne*, soft and cool-looking.'

'Oh—Jourdan!'

'Ah, Melly.' His eyes held hers as he raised his glass of champagne. 'Come, drink with me and just for tonight let us not ask questions of the moment, let us live it.'

'Very well, Jourdan.' She surrendered her will to his ... to the tense yet exciting atmosphere that was in the air. The hotel seemed caught in the eye of the storm, high above the bay as it was, a target for the thunder and lightning and the torrential roar of the rain.

Later that evening it wasn't unexpected that someone should suggest they make a party of it, and while the storm raged outside the music played inside.

A certain amount of danger has a way of adding a certain stimulus, and the dancing continued into the midnight hour, becoming dreamy and sentimental. Jourdan drew Melly close to him and she felt his hard jaw resting upon her hair. She moved with him through the rhythm of the dance, feeling as if they were locked together in a dream ... a perfect dream she longed to cling to.

'I thought you had no romance in you?' Jourdan commented.

'The storm and the champagne have made me light-headed,' she replied.

'And possibly light-hearted tonight?'

'Yes.' Her heart was beating fast beneath the chiffon of her dress, and suddenly she had to shatter the fragile dream or it would possess her. 'Can we sit out now, Jourdan? I'm feeling rather footworn and thirsty, and I'd love a glass of lemonade.'

'As you wish, *ma chère*.' He walked her to the glazed terrace where she watched the steely glare of the lightning and heard the howling of the wind. She would never forget this night, she told herself. The very drama of it was part of her realisation that she couldn't have what she longed for, a loving and lasting relationship with Jourdan. She touched a hand to her heart and felt the beat of it right against her fingertips. This was a night for lovers, exciting and elemental, and Melly had to deny herself to Jourdan when every beat of her heart was clamouring for his love.

She longed to be part of him . . . in truth she was part of him and always would be, but her body shrank from being possessed.

Jourdan returned with a pair of glasses on a tray. 'Try a Tom Collins,' he said. 'Gin and lemon.'

It was pleasant, especially the cool taste of the ice floating in the drink. They sat in terrace chairs, spectators of the storm, the vivid flashes lighting their faces for each other. The roll of the thunder was like the cannon of the gods.

'Glad that we stayed?'

'Yes.' Melly's smile was tinged with a little shadow. 'I think this has been the most significant night of my life.'

'For me it has also been very special. Melly, look at me.'

She carefully did so, composing her features even if she couldn't control her troubled and loving heart. As her eyes dwelt on his lean and distinctive face she wanted to reach out and stroke her fingers down his cheek.

'Do you believe, *mignonne*, that never with anyone else have I enjoyed myself so much? You have great capacity for enjoyment, do you know? Genuine, unspoilt enjoyment.'

'It's been like a party,' she murmured.

'And there have not been many parties for you, have there?'

'Oh, if you have too much of a good thing you become blasé.' As she spoke lightning seemed to lick against the glass near where she sat, white-silver flame that lit her skin and hair. As she caught her breath Jourdan seemed to do the same.

'I—I think I'd like to go to my room now, Jourdan. I'm starting to feel drowsy.'

'I shall come with you.'

They went upstairs in the lift and Melly stood quiet, avoiding Jourdan's eyes. She stepped out quickly when the lift stopped and the iron doors rattled open. She walked ahead of his tall figure and waited silently as he unlocked the door of their suite. Once inside she went quickly across to the door that led into her room.

'Goodnight, Jourdan,' she called over her shoulder. 'Thank you for a lovely evening.'

She closed the door quickly behind her and leaned against it . . . dear God, she hated herself for treating him like an acquaintance who had taken her out for the evening.

Sharp hot tears filled her eyes . . . she loved him so, and it hurt right through to the bone to have to shut a door in his face. The tears spilled over and fell down her face and all her joy in the evening seemed to drain away.

Half blinded by her tears, Melly blundered to the bedside where a box of paper handkerchiefs lay on the night table. She grabbed a handful and stood there crying like a sad, hurt child. All the banked-down pain of the past months welled up and burst the walls of her restraint.

Grievous tears that felt acid against her skin, worsening the wound rather than relieving it. Her private storm almost matched the one that battered at the walls and windows of the hotel, the ache still there inside her when half an hour later she climbed into bed and buried her face in the pillows.

Because the dancing and the crying had exhausted her she fell asleep quite soon and wasn't disturbed by the storm until it built to a crescendo about two o'clock in the morning, the force of the wind suddenly hurling open one of her window shutters and throwing it noisily against the wall.

Melly came awake with a startled cry, her body shaken by the noise of the shutter. She sat up in bed and stared across the room in the grip of a nervous reaction which had nothing to do with the abrupt opening of her bedroom door. She had been dreaming . . . reliving in her sleep happenings she had tried so often to forget.

Jourdan stood framed in the lamplight of his own room. 'I heard a crash—are you all right?' he demanded.

Melly felt the lurch of her heart when she saw him there, silhouetted tall and dark against the shaded light. 'I—I think a shutter has blown open—it banged against the wall a-and woke me up.'

'I had better fix it.' He strode to the window and she heard him fiddling with the latch, then the lightning was shut out as the shutter was closed. 'The latch has loosened and needs to be tied,' he said. 'I think I have some string in my jacket pocket.'

He returned to his room and Melly hugged the bedcovers around her, still in the grip of the wave of alarm which had swept over her. Sounds and scents, she thought, and the *déjà-vu* of a relived moment that brought back vividly the details which time blurred.

Jourdan came back into her room and she watched as he set about securing the shutter so it wouldn't be forced open again. The task attended to he came to her bedside and stood looking down at her in the stream of light from his room.

'That must have scared you, the way you cried out. It reminded me of that other time . . . are you subject to nightmares, Melly?'

'Not often.' She managed a smile. 'It was the shutter banging open—I thought a thunderbolt had flown through the window.'

'Are you going to be all right?' Jourdan sat down casually on the side of her bed and she could see that he was bare-chested and wearing only the trousers of his pyjamas; paisley silk ones which he had bought at the same time as the filmy nightdress she was wearing, and which she was attempting to hide with the bedcovers.

'I'll be fine,' she assured him. 'You can go back to bed now, Jourdan, and thank you for fixing the shutter.'

'You speak as if you can't wait to see the back

of me.' He thrust a hand through his hair and made it even more tousled, and the glint in his eyes was not one of amusement as they strayed over her face and down to where the covers were clutched against her.

'All tonight, Melly, I have been thinking that our marriage has been a kind of catharsis for both of us.' He spoke carefully, as if her attention was a bird he mustn't startle into flight. 'You and I are duty bound to make something of our lives, and I think we should start to do it right now.'

Melly had started to shake her head even before he stopped speaking. 'No, Jourdan, we can't——'

'That is a negative way to look at it, *mignonne*. The reasons that led to our marriage have become null and void, but that does not mean that our marriage is no longer a reality. You are here, I am here, and between us we can make substance out of shadow.'

With the same coaxing care with which he spoke Jourdan took hold of the covers that Melly was using as a shield, and as he did this the shaft of lamplight showed the terror that filled her eyes. 'No—please don't, Jourdan! Y-you promised——'

'So did you, Melly. Only this morning you promised to help me make a good thing of the plantation, and when I spoke about putting down roots you listened to me, you agreed that I should, and you know very well what a man implies when he talks about roots.' His fingers gripped her flimsy shield. 'I want us to have a child, Melly. I want a child to replace Jody . . . you know I've lost her! You must realise that!'

'Yes——' Melly was trembling as once before

she had trembled when a man had sat on the side
of her bed ... not a lean, dark-haired man whom
she loved but a far more fearful figure who had
spoken words that went through her like a knife.

'No,' she had cried out, 'you can't do it—you
can't!'

In a whisper she repeated her words, and with a
face as adamant as if cast in bronze Jourdan
leaned down to her and with fingers firm as iron
he pulled aside the covers. 'Yes, *mon amour*,' he
said softly, and his eyes held hers ... held them
with a silver blaze that magnetized her.

'I can't—have your baby,' she whispered.

'My sweet-faced Melly, you have very little
choice.' His hands gathered her close against him
and his lips were in her soft warm hair.

Melly felt the touch of him, so strong and so
vitally alive in his every fibre ... a man fit only
for a woman who had a lovely, perfect body to
give him his joy ... and his child.

Gritting her teeth, she took his hand and
carried it to where her heart beat heavily beneath
the diagonal line of faded stitching where her left
breast had been. She pressed his fingers there,
making him feel the faint ridge of the scar,
waiting like a frightened little animal for his
rejection of her disfigurement.

Instead he held her fast ... he held her and
rocked her and whispered her name over and
over again, in a deep voice that thrilled her
through and through.

'Everything is all right, my dearest Melly. I
have known for several days—*mon Dieu*, don't
jump like that or you will do yourself an injury!'

His large hand stroked her hair. 'Bethula came
to me and told me in the good, kind way that she

has. She soon realised how things stood between us, then in her wisdom came to understand why you kept yourself out of my arms. Ah, Melly, as if I would not want you in my arms! Did you not guess when we danced together? Did you not feel how I wanted you? Don't you know that I have grown to love you very much?'

A sob broke from Melly. 'I—I thought you would mind—about the way I am.'

'Mind?' He pressed her to him as if he wanted to absorb her into his flesh and bones. 'I love *you*, not your shape! It is *you* I want, not just a female body with all the parts intact.'

His hands framed her face and with a tender fierceness he kissed her lips. 'I don't know when it began. Perhaps from the moment they pumped your blood into my veins because when you came into my sickroom I couldn't take my eyes from you. Then each time I looked at you, each time I tried to touch you, you had such a look in your eyes that I felt a brute. At that time I failed to understand your fear and thought it was of the kind that fades as a girl becomes used to a man. Then Bethula came to me and told me what was wrong. You wear a prosthesis, don't you, so your figure appears normal beneath your clothing. Bethula saw it in its pink box and finally came to me in tears.'

'Oh, Jourdan,' Melly buried her face in his shoulder, 'I didn't want you to think me ugly.'

'*Mon amour*, as if I would! You with such hair, such a gentle heart, such depth after the shallowness of Irene! What on earth made you believe such a thing of me?'

'At the time I had the operation, when my body was all bruised from the cutting, one of the nurses——' Melly swallowed to ease her throat, 'she said it was something she'd rather die than have done to her, because a man would find it so shocking—so impossible to accept.'

Jourdan cursed in his own language, and his strong arms enclosed her so that through the bars of bone she could feel their heartbeats blending. 'Now, do I seem shocked?' he fiercely asked.

'No.' She said it tentatively. 'I—I don't want your pity, Jourdan.'

'I am not a very pitying person, my love.' He tilted her face to him, his fingers hard against her skull, through the blonde softness of her hair. His eyes were commanding in their love for her. 'Now you are going to tell me how it happened, then never again shall we speak of it. Agreed?'

'But, Jourdan,' a flush warmed her skin, 'how can I have a baby—how would I manage to feed the little mite?'

'My darling,' he laughed softly, 'if we do happen to have twins, then we shall arrange the feeding bottle on this side.' And baring the thin white scar and bending his head, he ran his lips from top to bottom of it. 'We shall make a little sling to hold the bottle, how does that sound?'

Melly felt herself smiling, and all at once inhibition and doubt were gone and she wanted to be as near to him as she could get. 'Come into bed with me,' she implored, and without a moment's hesitation he joined her in the warm bed and drew her all the way into his arms. She hadn't dreamed, hadn't known that a man so outwardly tough could be so innately tender. She felt that tenderness flowing through the muscular arms that held her so close to him . . . felt the desire that was for her, a person very dear to him.

Her heart overflowed and for a little while longer she couldn't speak of the agony which had held them apart.

Then in a while, in the soft and trusting tones of intimacy, Melly told him of the accident which had happened at the riding-school that summer afternoon when all had seemed so carefree, the sky blue and gold, the birds twittering along the lanes where the hedgerows were heavy with blossom.

In the summertime they were always busy at the school; there were holidaymakers to mount and so extra girls were hired to help out. But apart from the people on holiday who wanted to ride there were always the regulars, one of them a local resident for whom a special horse was always set aside. He had a disability, but riding was dear to him, and a gentle mare was always kept free for him.

But that afternoon one of the new girls mounted him on the wrong horse and because the man's disabled leg made him rather clumsy the less patient horse became fractuous. With a sudden bellow it had thrown the man to the ground, where he lay helplessly in danger of being trampled.

'I dashed across to help——' Melly shivered at the memory, 'and the horse lashed out at me——'

'And you took the full force of an iron-shod hoof in your breast!' As Jourdan spoke he gripped Melly against his heart, as if to absorb her memory of the pain into himself, where his strength might dilute it.

'Yes,' she said, remembering how the agony of the blow had sent her reeling back against one of the stalls, where she had clung to the half-shutter for a sickening moment, until she slid to the ground where the acrid tang of the straw kept her conscious for hideously long moments, hardly knowing if it was she who screamed or the girl who had unwittingly caused the accident.

Melly trembled in her husband's arms as she recounted all of it, the swift journey by ambulance to the hospital, the siren wailing. Her awakening from the operation, the black bruising and dark despair . . . her left breast amputated, her slim young figure never to be trim and sure again in a riding outfit.

'I—I could never bear to ride after that,' she said quietly. 'My nerve with horses had gone, so when I had convalesced I moved to London and it seemed somehow natural to go and work in a hospital, to be among people who had things wrong with them. For a while when I was with other young women I—I felt—left out. It was a strange kind of feeling, and I couldn't seem to forget what that nurse had said to me. Whenever I looked at myself in a mirror I felt sure she was right, to say that a man would be shocked, so I began to keep to myself. It seemed safer. I couldn't be hurt again—and then—then you came along.'

'And I shall never go away, God willing.' Jourdan cradled her and his lips travelled all over her face. 'Dear, brave Melly, you are so precious to me—doubly so now I know all about you. How I want you, my Melandra! May I have you?'

Oh, they were such heavenly words, and they filled her heart with a reciprocal longing. 'Jourdan,' she stroked his face and it was so exciting to see his smouldering eyes upon her, 'you are so real and strong and warm, and I do love you so—listen, the thunder has died away and the storm is over.'

'No, sweetheart,' he laughed softly, 'the storm is just about to begin.'

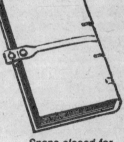

Your FREE gift includes
- MAN OF POWER by **Mary Wibberley**
- THE WINDS OF WINTER by **Sandra Field**
- THE LEO MAN by **Rebecca Stratton**
- LOVE BEYOND REASON by **Karen van der Zee**

FREE GIFT CERTIFICATE

and Subscription Reservation

Mail this coupon today!

Harlequin Reader Service

In the U.S.A.
2504 West Southern Ave.
Tempe, AZ 85282

In Canada
P.O. Box 2800, Postal Station A
5170 Yonge Street,
Willowdale, Ont. M2N 6J3

Please send me my 4 Harlequin Romance novels FREE.
Also, reserve a subscription to the 6 NEW Harlequin
Romance novels published each month. Each month I will
receive 6 NEW Romance novels at the low price of $1.50
each (*Total–$9.00 a month*). There are no shipping and
handling or any other hidden charges. I may cancel this
arrangement at any time, but even if I do, these first 4 books
are still mine to keep.   116 BPR EAUC

NAME   (PLEASE PRINT)

ADDRESS   APT. NO.

CITY

STATE/PROV.   ZIP/POSTAL CODE

This offer is limited to one order per household and not valid to
current *Harlequin Romance* subscribers. We reserve the right
to exercise discretion in granting membership.
Offer expires September 30, 1985
® ™ Trademarks of Harlequin Enterprises Ltd.   R-SUB-2US

If price changes are necessary you will be notified

Get this book FREE!

Mail to:
Harlequin Reader Service

In the U.S.
2504 West Southern Ave.
Tempe, AZ 85282

In Canada
P.O. Box 2800, Postal Station A
5170 Yonge St., Willowdale, Ont. M2N 6J3

YES! I want to be one of the first to discover **Harlequin American Romance.** Send me FREE and without obligation *Twice in a Lifetime.* If you do not hear from me after I have examined my FREE book, please send me the 4 new **Harlequin American Romances** each month as soon as they come off the presses. I understand that I will be billed only $2.25 for each book (total $9.00). There are no shipping or handling charges. There is no minimum number of books that I have to purchase. In fact, I may cancel this arrangement at any time. *Twice in a Lifetime* is mine to keep as a FREE gift, even if I do not buy any additional books.   154 BPA NAZE

Name   (please print)

Address   Apt. no.

City   State/Prov.   Zip/Postal Code

Signature (If under 18, parent or guardian must sign.)

AMR-SUB-2